Knucklehead & Other Stories

W. Mark Giles

ANVIL PRESS | VANCOUVER

Knucklehead & Other Stories
Copyright © 2003 by W. Mark Giles

National Library of Canada Cataloguing in Publication Data

Giles, W. Mark

Knucklehead, and other stories / W. Mark Giles.

ISBN 1-895636-50-7

I. Title.
PS8563.I4763K58 2003   C813'.6   C2003-910173-8
PR9199.4.G54K58 2003

Printed and bound in Canada
Cover by Rayola Graphic Design
Typesetting by HeimatHouse

Represented in Canada by the Literary Press Group
Distributed by the University of Toronto Press

The publisher gratefully acknowledges the financial assistance of the B.C. Arts Council, the Canada Council for the Arts, and the Book Publishing Industry Development Program (BPIDP) for their support of our publishing program.

Anvil Press
6 West 17th Avenue
Vancouver, B.C. V5Y 1Z4   CANADA
www.anvilpress.com

For Secord

Acknowledgements

I offer my deepest gratitude to my partner Donna Sharpe, who anchors me to the world. And to my daughter Lucy Piper, who teaches me something new every day about how we shape the world with language and story. I love you (both) madly.

I am forever grateful to Fred Stenson of the Banff Centre's Wired Writing Program and Aritha van Herk at the University of Calgary: their expert, incisive, and unfailingly accurate guidance made these stories into a book. I owe many thanks to my English 598 peers at the University of Calgary for their readings, insight, and support. Reverend Aurelian Giles gave me counsel that allowed me to seek permission from myself not to write for some years; Edna Alford at two different times gave me the encouragement to continue. Thanks too to Carol Holmes and the staff at the Banff Centre Writing and Publishing Program for their dedication to nurturing a space for creative work.

I have benefited from those in writing groups who have been my patient first readers – thank you especially to Belle Auld, Ross Deegan, and Pat Hastings. For his unflagging belief in my writing, I thank Ameen Merchant. For affirming my faith that people read, I thank my book discussion group: Bob Banks, Tim Breitkreutz, Debbie Brooks, and Annette De Jong.

Many thanks to Brian Kaufman and Jenn Farrell at Anvil Press, whose unflagging work, attention to detail, and passion for publishing have transformed the imaginary into the material book you hold in your hands.

Versions of some of these stories have appeared previously: "K," "Tears of the Waiter Soup," and excerpts from "Fugue for Solo Cello and Barking Dogs" in *subTerrain*; "Remission" in *The Antigonish Review*; "Cigarettes" and "Al's Book of the Dead" in *Canadian Fiction Magazine*; "Industrial Accidents," "The Man in the CAT Hat," and "Towards a Semiosis of Two-headed Dog" in *The New Quarterly*; "The Day the Buffalo Came" in *NeWest Review*; "Sweetwater" in *The Malahat Review*; "Thanksgiving" in *blue buffalo*; "Wrestlemania" in *Grain*.

CONTENTS

K

The boy in the field. Is he tow-headed? Carrot-topped? Freckled? Olive-skinned? Cow-eyed? Wall-eyed? One-eyed? Is the boy white? A possibility: the boy lies on his back in a fallow field beyond the edge of town. Perhaps he chews kernels of raw wheat into prairie gum. Scudding clouds hypothesize representational shapes. On a distant ridge, a question-mark of smoke smudges the sky with the lingering threat of a grass fire. The sun may burn, yellow-eyed, edging towards one horizon or another. Imagine the boy's pockets full of potash.

■　　■　　■

A hired man takes a break from the toil of twisting an auger to dig a hole for a gate post. He pulls his hat from his head, wipes his brow with a forearm. He walks and fetches the canteen full of water, covered in wet burlap and hung on the outside rearview mirror of his truck. After drinking three long draughts, he soaks his hat. He settles the canteen into the crook of his neck, and rests his cheek against it.

◼   ◼   ◼

At night, under the patchwork frenzy quilted by grandmother's arthritic fingers, the boy curls around a pillow. Transistor radio held tight to his ear, he listens to hillbilly music from a station in North Carolina. In an abandoned farmhouse in the fallow field, hundreds, thousands of bluebottle flies lie dead on the floor. He catches a garter snake, keeps it in a mason jar covered with a burlap remnant until it escapes. At the shore of the lake—more slough than lake—every flat rock is potentially an arrowhead. The boy turns each one in his hands, then skips it across the water. What does potash look like?

◼   ◼   ◼

The hired man takes a cigarette from a tin box he keeps in his pocket. He dangles it from the corner of his mouth, where a cigarette always dangles, so that his left eye has a permanent squint from closing against the smoke. He cups his hand around the Zippo and flicks the flint wheel. Squatting in the scant shade of the truck, he takes deep inhalations of tobacco smoke. He thinks about his children: "Just stepping out for a deck of smokes." How old would the boy be now?

◼   ◼   ◼

Rodeo bulls bursting through the gate, smashing fences, stampeding the crowd. The boy buys Coca-Cola in a six-ounce bottle. He tucks the green glass into the crook between cheek and shoulder, the way his dad used to do with stubby brown bottles of Bohemian Maid.

◼   ◼   ◼

The hired man hauls himself to his feet and plucks the cigarette from his mouth. He flicks it aside and the wind carries the glowing butt into the tall grass. He grips the handles of the auger and bends his back to the dig.

◼   ◼   ◼

Father has gone to Saskatoon to work in the potash mine. Standing between rows of ripening corn, the boy stares down between his feet into the dark earth, a mile down through topsoil, the clay mantle, granite bedrock, through underground rivers teeming with blind pale fish, through layers of rock flowing in the push of earth lifting the fossilized dinosaurs in their tide, he stares down into the earth, searching, searching, searching for potash.

Remission

—I like it here, she said to her lemon tree. In the bright light of the morning sun, in the cosy kitchen away from the outside cold, the lemon tree seemed happy to agree: I'm glad you like it here. Joanne cupped a palm under each leaf and cleaned it with a damp cloth. The lemon tree flourished, it sprouted deep green, luxuriant, shiny leaves. Joanne didn't wash the new ones.

A lazy winter fly circled overhead, then gained altitude in a looping spiral.

—Why are you here? Joanne said. She retrieved the flyswatter from its hook beneath the sink. It had an old-fashioned wire handle, twisted like a doctor's two snakes, with a rubber striking pad not quite the same colour as the walls. Scrub green, Joanne called it, like a hospital gown.

She swiped at the fly as it circled the light fixture. The fly accelerated. Joanne waited. If flies have all those eyes, why can't they see where they're going? Imagine running full speed in a room with many angles, bumping surfaces again and again, just like the fly was doing. It stopped suddenly, a couple of inches below the ceiling in the corner where two walls met.

—You don't belong here, Joanne said to the fly. She pulled over the stool with the folding step that she used to reach high cupboards. Even standing on the stool, it was a long reach. The fly waited. Slowly she brought the head of the swatter to a position four or five inches from the fly. She flicked her wrist and struck.

The tip of the swatter deflected off the ceiling. The fly swerved through the kitchen and stopped above the telephone nook. Joanne repositioned the stool to its usual place, where she sat when she talked long-distance to her mother. She stepped up quickly and swung. Missed. The fly buzzed slowly around the room.

—Well come on, you stupid fly, Joanne said. The fly buzzed back at her. She lost sight of it momentarily as she tried to track its course. It came to rest over the sink, lower on the wall. Completely still. She swung with a full arm movement and killed it.

—About time, she said. The fly stuck to the wall. She used a tissue to remove it, then wiped the spot clean.

She put the flyswatter away, rinsed the cloth, then lingered at the sink, gazing out the window. Her two boys — aged five and four, just eleven months apart — frolicked in the trampled snow of the yard. Bundled in their banana-yellow and tangerine snowsuits, the children looked alien in the white landscape.

—And my children, Joanne said. The spider plant swung in its macramé hanger, the azalea on the fridge fluttered slightly from a blast of furnace air, all the house plants seemed to nod their understanding.

She couldn't hear their shouts and cries, saw only their breath burst from their mouths and hang frozen in the air. Benjamin hopped on his one leg, steadying himself with a hand on the pole of the swing set. He waved one of his aluminum crutches in the other hand, fending off his brother. Jason knocked aside the crutch and pushed Benjamin down, then sat astride him. He dropped a handful of snow on his younger brother's face. Sam the Samoyed ran to and fro.

—And my dog, Joanne said. She wiped the windowsill, lifting the three-inch pots of African violets and nasturtiums, checking for water marks.

■   ■   ■

An hour later, Benjamin was teasing his older brother, mimicking his every move. He drank his stove-warmed Nestlé Quik, matching the way Jason licked his lips, imitating the satisfied Aah! after every sip. Joanne looked away and concentrated on the piece of black hashish she was crumbling on the trivet. Beautiful hashish.

She scorched the hashish with her Cricket lighter, just to the point where it smouldered, then mulched it finely with her thumbnail and forefinger. Green really, not black, greener on the inside where the air couldn't darken it. Sticky with resin. Somebody told her that they made some kinds of hash by running naked through fields of marijuana, allowing the resin to cling to their bodies, then rubbing it off and rolling it into balls. Joanne raised her fingers to her face and inhaled the pungent scent of hemp. All the way from Afghanistan or Kathmandu or

Tibet or Timbuktu. Clean, sharp, vegetable smell. Strong. She and Dale had smoked a joint at six that morning, before he went to work. She rocked back and forth in time to the Peter Tosh anthem unspiralling from the record player in the living room. *Legalize it, yeah, yeah, yeah.* She would smoke some more.

—Hey Mom, are we going to the mall today? asked Jason.

—Hey Mom, are we going to the mall today?

—Cut it out. [*elbow*]

—Cut it out. [*elbow-elbow*]

—Both of you cut it out, Joanne said without looking up. She mixed the pile of hashish with tobacco from the half-cigarette Dale had left for her.

—Yes, we're going to the mall. She pulled a rolling paper from the package of blue Zig-Zags and spread some of the mixture into the crease of the thin leaf. The mall is where we always go. Enough for two joints. Two mind-blowing joints.

It was a downer to smoke dope alone. She wished Dale would somehow come home and surprise her. But he's gone to Keephills today, to work on some boiler or something. She wished he would feel her need and drive home and be here and they would smoke a joint together, they would make wild love right after, set the kids up with Bugs Bunny on the new Betamax, and retreat to their waterbed to find the rhythm of their bodies, rising together to an amazing hashish orgasm. Then smoke the other joint and do it all again.

—The mall with the rides, Mom? I wanna go on the train, Jason said.

—The mall with the rides—

16

Benjamin cut short the mimicking with a cry. Jason pounded his arm three times.

—Stop [*smack*] copying [*smack*] me [*smack*].

A balled cloth sailed across the kitchen and knocked over a mug. Not-so-hot chocolate splattered over the table, over Jason, mostly over Benjamin. Benjamin's crocodile tears faltered for an instant, followed by genuine ones. Jason looked agape at his mother.

—You threw the rag, Mom.

—Yes I did, Joanne said. She brushed the last of her hash-tobacco mixture into a second fold of paper, rolled it quickly between her fingers, and flicked her tongue across the glued edge. Benjamin bawled. He held his hands up, his face turned red.

—Jason, wipe the table. Hurry, it's dripping on the floor. Joanne walked over to the boys and fussed over Benjamin. Jason pushed the spilled drink into the middle of the table, corralling it with the cloth. Nestlé Quik flecked the leaves of the coleus. I must clean that before I go out, Joanne thought.

—Hey Mom, can I ride on the train? Jason asked. Joanne tried to pick up Benjamin. He had quieted, but as she worked her arms behind his knee and under his arms, he went limp.

—C'mon, you've got to help your mommy. You're too big for mommy to carry without help. Please Benjy, I'll clean you all up.

He lifted his arms around his mother's neck, and shifted his weight to fold into her. Joanne unbent her back to lift him from the chair. She took him in her arms towards the bathroom.

—Can I ride the train? asked Benjamin.

■   ■   ■

Wrapped into one of Dale's old parkas, Joanne trudged down the road, pushing Benjamin in the stroller. She had left his prosthesis at home. Benjamin didn't like his new leg. It was bigger and heavier than the one he had outgrown, harder to work the knee, and he complained it hurt, especially in the cold. It was a hassle to strap on. He had long outgrown the stroller, but it made the winter walk go faster. He was too slow on the crutches. They walked in the centre of the street, where the grader had cleared a path.

A small snow lump sailed past to Joanne's left. She saw it, but didn't turn. Jason dawdled behind, sulking, throwing snow. Joanne had eighteen one-dollar bills in her purse, maybe three or four more dollars in change. Dale would get a cheque in three days, he would give her some money. There were Christmas bills, payments on the stereo and the furniture, but he should give her a hundred at least. Then they could take the bus—even a taxi—to the big mall, and Jason could have his ride on the train. But for now it was her Woolco card and the budget mall within walking distance. Another snow lump skittered by. If he hits me, Joanne thought.

She had smoked one of the joints before leaving home (the other one was tucked away with rolling papers and lighter in an old lozenge tin in her purse). The stone was heavy. She was aware of her body, the sting of winter in her cheeks, the heaviness of each arm, each leg, as she pushed Benjamin along, the screech of frozen wheels bearing too much weight. She melded into the day, into the scrunch-scrunch of boots and snow that measured each step, the flex of muscle to bring each foot forward. Eyes half-closed against the needling wind and the

18

glare of sunlight, she forgot the bills, the bickering with Dale, the oven that needed cleaning. She forgot her dreams of a cabin in the woods, tropical suns, her fantasies of desire, she forgot the name of the disease that claimed Benjamin's leg, that waited in the bone to be renamed with every visit to the doctor, she forgot her conversations with house plants, the long minutes spent at the kitchen window feeling a weight in her gut, watching her children and dog in the yard. There was only the cold and snow and the sound of steps and the squealing wheels and the motion of her limbs and the warm molasses bath that was slow and sweet in her brain.

Jason tossed another lump of snow that hit Joanne square on the back of the head.

■   ■   ■

At the mall, Joanne unbundled the boys, stowed the snowsuits and her jacket in a neat package on the seat of the stroller. Jason dashed off to peek through the doors of a hobby shop. Benjamin complained that his missing leg hurt. He sat on a bench and rubbed the end of his stump through his pants. She knew not to ask questions: phantom pain confused him. He might start to cry. The doctor said confusion was normal. How can it hurt when it's not there? She said:

—Let's check you out. She took a quick look around. Tuesday, no big sales at the mall, thirty below outside, 10 a.m. Not a soul in sight. She tucked her fingers into Benjamin's waistband and pulled his drawers down.

—Mom, don't, Benjamin said, grabbing at his pants.

—Don't worry, Benjy. No one can see us. She unwound the elastic bandage that wrapped his thigh. She rolled the stump-sock down, and vigorously massaged his flesh.

—Ow. Mommy, that's too hard, Benjamin said. Joanne felt his cold skin. She had probably wrapped the bandage too tightly. Dale was always saying she wrapped it too tightly or too loosely. His leg was always cold or swollen. It was never just right.

—It's not hard. That's better isn't it? she said. She watched the circulation returning, as the surface of the skin turned red from her rubbing. The thigh tapered to a blunt point. She caressed the nub, and leaned close to cast her warm breath into the cup of her hands.

—Someone's coming, Jason said. He had come up behind where Benjamin sat, looking past his mother's shoulder to the door that led to the parking lot. Joanne hiked up Benjamin's pants over the stump and the unravelled bandage. An elderly couple entered, stamped the snow from their boots, and moved slowly down the mall. Their rubber overshoes squeaked on the terrazzo floor. Then she exposed the leg again, pulled the sock on, and rewrapped the bandage.

—Does that feel too tight? she asked. Benjamin shook his head. Too loose? Another shake, a shrug.

—Okay, she said, that does it. She checked the safety pin holding his trouser leg tucked up under his knee. She unpacked the crutches that were lashed to the stroller handle with an elastic cord and handed them to Benjamin. He pulled himself up from the bench.

—Hey, look at this, said Jason, running down the mall. Benjamin followed, almost keeping up. Joanne pushed the stroller piled with winter clothes, stopping at the display window of Peoples Jewellers.

■   ■   ■

Joanne used her credit card at the luncheonette in Woolco. Mrs. Bell, her neighbour from across the alley, entered and sat at the table beside them. Mrs. Bell worked in the Saan store at the other end of the mall: it was her lunch break. Joanne could never remember her first name. Gladys? Beryl?

—How is he? Mrs. Bell said, pointing with a nod and a flick of her eyes towards Benjamin. She took a wax-paper package from her purse, placed it on the formica tabletop, and briskly unwrapped it.

—He's fine, Joanne said. Total remission. Did she say that or just think it? She watched a coarse black hair that grew from a mole on the older woman's chin. It moved up and down as Mrs. Bell chewed the white bread and variety meat. The effects of the hashish had dulled to a comfortable fatigue, a pleasant fuzziness. Joanne spooned tomato soup into her mouth so she wouldn't have to say anything. She knew Mrs. Bell would fill the silence.

—Morris's brother had his gallstones out last month, Mrs. Bell said. This is Myron, his older brother, what lives out in Stony Plain. And instead of getting better and better, he just got sicker. The doctors and nurses fussed around. Finally they took him back into surgery, after three days mind you. What do you think they found?

Joanne sipped more soup. Too salty.

—A sponge, Mrs. Bell said. They found a sponge. Some dumb

nurse left a sponge inside him. What do you think of that?

Joanne imagined a sponge in her gall bladder. Where is the gall bladder? How different does a sponge feel from a stone?

—I tell them they should call my Jamie. He's the lawyer. Call Jamie, I go, send him after that darn hospital. Mrs. Bell took another bite of sandwich, chewed three or four times before she continued: But they wouldn't. They're just happy it's all okay now. Some people.

—Benjamin, stop that, Joanne said. He was fingerpainting with his chili con carne.

—It's a pitcher of you, he said. A circle with two dots for eyes, a little crescent nose and a smiling mouth.

—Eat your lunch, Joanne said. Don't play with your food.

—I'm full, he said. I ate my hotdog.

Joanne wetted a paper napkin in her stainless steel teapot, cleaned the sauce from Benjamin's hand, then cleaned the table.

—Jason, do you want the rest of Benjy's chili?

Jason looked at his mom, belched, and grinned hugely.

—No thanks, Mom, Jason said. Can I go watch that man play Pac-Man?

—Sure, Joanne said. Go on. She pulled the blue-edged bowl towards her.

Mrs. Bell was reminiscing about her hysterectomy. Her monthly visits were so bad, she felt she was dying.

—You girls have it lucky now, Mrs. Bell said. What with female doctors and all. When I was young . . .

Joanne watched the boys move off to the video games by the exit. Jason skipped on ahead, Benjamin hopped after, holding both crutches in one hand. She ate the chili. It was too salty too.

—A Filter Queen, maybe, Mrs. Bell said. Joanne had missed the transition, but nodded.

—The lady said I get fifty dollars worth of dry cleaning certificates. Guaranteed hundred dollar trade-in on my old machine. Just to watch a demonstration. How do you like that?

—I got an Electrolux for Christmas, Joanne said. Joanne liked her vacuum. It was powerful, with a beater bar, and accessories for crevices and drapes that fit into a neat little box. It reminds me of a dog.

—What's that? Mrs. Bell said.

—My Electrolux. It reminds me of a little wiener dog, Joanne said. You know, long and low.

—A dachshund, Mrs. Bell said. Morris's brother and his new wife, they have dachshunds. Not the Myron with the gall bladder, this is Martin, lives in Montreal. The old one, Gertie they call her, she wears a diaper. Imagine that, a dog with a diaper.

—Mom, Mom. Jason came running over. Can I play Pac-Man?

—Mom, can I play? Benjamin said, three steps behind.

—No, Joanne said. She rose from her chair. It was nice seeing you Mrs. Bell. I have to get these guys home.

—Alice, Mrs. Bell said.

—What? Joanne said.

—I'm Alice. Not Mrs. Bell. It sounds so old. We're neighbours.

—Right. Okay. Alice. Joanne gathered her purse.

—How's your husband? Mrs. Bell asked.

—Fine, great, Joanne said. She put her purse in the stroller.

—I see him going off in the morning, Mrs. Bell said. Or if I don't see him, I hear him. That contraption of his is a noisy thing.

—It's a welding rig, Joanne said. Just a truck really. He's a welder. She gripped the stroller handles. He leaves early to get to the job sites. Like he's working out at Keephills this week.

—Morris is always going on how it's illegal to have a business in a residential area, Mrs. Bell said. But really, I go, they're our neighbours. You're such a nice young family. And you've got troubles enough. Mrs. Bell looked at Joanne, then at the boys. They had grown silent, crowding their mother's legs. They looked at Mrs. Bell's chin.

—Let me give the boys a quarter, Mrs. Bell said.

—No, really, Mrs. . . . . Alice. I wish you wouldn't.

—Yay! Yay! The boys surrounded Mrs. Bell on either side. Can I have two? Jason asked.

—I'll just give you one and you can share it, Mrs. Bell said, poking around in her boxy black vinyl handbag. Here you go. She placed the quarter in Benjamin's hand. He closed his fist on it.

—Gimme that, Jason said.

—Now boys, Joanne said. Share. Really, Mrs. Bell, I wish you wouldn't.

—Alice, Mrs. Bell said. Benjamin was hunched over, trying to protect the coin from Jason's prying fingers.

—Hey. Hey, Joanne said. Be nice. What do you say to Mrs. Bell? Jason. Benjamin. The boys kept struggling until Joanne came over and grabbed them lightly by their collars. What do you say?

—I'm sorry? Benjamin said. Mrs. Bell laughed.

—You're sorry? Mrs. Bell said.

—Not sorry, Benjamin. Say thank you, Joanne said.

—Thank you? Benjamin mumbled and dropped his head.

—Thanks, Mrs. Bell, Jason said. He looked at her and smiled. His hand quickly went out as he tried to catch Benjamin off-guard to take the quarter.

—Oh look, Mrs. Bell said. I have another one in my sweater. She held out another coin. Jason snatched it.

He turned and made for Pac-Man. Thanks a lot, he called back. Benjamin put his quarter in his mouth, slid his arms into the crutch braces and followed. Joanne smiled at Mrs. Bell, then looked down at the stroller.

—Thank you, she said. Alice.

—Oh, it's nothing. That poor little boy. Why in the world?

—Mom. Help me, Jason called. He was putting his quarter into the coin-return slot.

—Well, good-bye, Joanne said.

—Boys will be boys, Mrs. Bell said. Lord knows, I had three of them. She waved her hand, shook her head and smiled.

Joanne inserted the quarter for Jason, then played the first man for him, to show him what to do. He caught on quickly, manoeuvering the yellow blob through the maze. Joanne stared at the screen, listened to the electronic jingle. I will go home, she thought. I will settle the kids in front of the TV. I will vacuum the dog hair from under the couch and by the back door. I will get Benjamin's leg on. Dale likes to see Benjamin wearing his leg. I will take a meatloaf out of the freezer, and I will make a Duncan Hines layer cake. I will smoke that joint.

Cigarettes

Stinky Bob smelled bad. When Soupy—Mr. Campbell—told me to go find Bob, I just followed my nose. At a quarter after eight in the morning Soupy himself had come over the intercom to announce a staff meeting in the coffee room. I usually worked Zone 2 (electrical, ignition, brake and suspension systems, nuts and bolts, lots of the little stuff) and the coffee room is just up the stairs, so I was there quick and lit up a smoke.

Tattoo Terri came in right after, moved in on me like always, crushing her boobs against my arm. With one hand she scratched the back of my neck under my hair—I was pretty touchy about my hair back then, when I still had some—and like by instinct I pulled away. She was waiting for that, already had a hold of my cigarettes. So when I moved away, the pack just came right out of my pocket in her other hand. Before I could make a grab for them. "Hey Walter, can I bum a *fag*." "Fag" like it was some big joke, as usual.

"Jeez, Terri, why don't you buy your own once in a while." I could hear myself whining, and I wished I could think of some quick comeback like Danny would have. Tattoo Terri never grabbed Danny's smokes, and if she tried he'd say something smart.

"Take a Valium, Walter," she said. Pulled a Zippo from her smock pocket and lit up—she never had her own cigarettes, but she carried a gold-plated Zippo. Go figure. "You'd be all right if you ever got laid," Tattoo Terri said, blowing smoke towards the exhaust vent in the ceiling. The rose tattooed on her hand had a stem running from her wrist into full bloom between thumb and forefinger. It fluttered like a weird bird. She waved her hand a bit, flicking ash into an empty cardboard coffee cup.

"I been laid," I said.

"I *have* been laid," Tattoo Terri said.

"You too, huh?" I said back. I wished somebody else, Danny, was there to hear that one.

"You should use proper English. Say 'been' to rhyme with 'seen,' not 'sin.'" She was rubbing her earlobe now, where another tiny rose was tattooed where you might expect to see an earring. "Anyway, I'm sure you have. Been laid." She took a long inhale and flexed her forearm, where there was a parrot as colourful as a bunch of flowers. She blew smoke in my face to make me look up, then finished: "But your daddy doesn't count."

I gave her the finger. "I'll have to trust you on that one," I said.

She watched the parrot as it ruffled its feathers on her arm. "Yep, you will."

Everyone else started coming into the coffee room. The whole warehouse staff, guys from the front office and sales reps. They even closed down the order desk. I just sat back and tried to enjoy my smoke. Didn't usually have a chance to sneak one between starting time and coffee break. Finally Soupy came in. Only Danny and Bob were missing.

Soupy was a jerk in a harmless sort of way. He was the boss, right? Wasn't much older than Danny, or even me for that matter, maybe five or seven years, fresh out of business college and into the warehouse. Always trying to act like one of the crew, a pat on the back, a soft jab to the shoulder. Telling a bad joke we'd already seen in the morning paper. Then all that touchy-feely stuff—"We're all managers here," or "Never say, 'It's not my job.'" Worst of all, helping out when things got busy—picking orders, packing boxes, checking shipments. Then we'd spend the next week fixing his screw-ups for customers he'd pissed off. Today wasn't going to be any pep talk, that was for sure. He shoved his hands in his pockets, pulling the shoulders of his jacket low. One of those fake hunting jackets, tweed or whatever with a suede patch over the right shoulder, like he was going to go shoot some ducks and drink sherry at noon hour. He went around the room, kind of fidgety, shifting his weight from foot to foot, jerking his head around, not actually looking at any of us.

"Where's Bob?" he said to me, like I had all the answers.

"Probably in Zone 4," I said. Stinky Bob never came to the coffee room. If he did, everyone else left. Well, Tattoo Terri stayed.

"Walter," Soupy said, "go get Bob." It was the closest thing to a direct order I ever heard him give.

I had to make a quick decision. Butt my smoke and save it for later, or just leave it burning and hope to get a couple of puffs off it when I got back. "What about Danny?" I asked. Enough time for one more drag.

"Danny," Soupy said. Started to fidget again. He turned to Tattoo Terri and out of the blue asked her for a cigarette.

"Walter has some," she said. Gave me a "gotcha" look.

"Sure," I said, fished my pack out of my pocket. How could I say no to my boss, even if he didn't smoke. His hand shook a bit as he took one. Tattoo Terri held out her Zippo and flicked the flame on, but he didn't light up right away. "Walter, would you please find Bob and ask him if he would like to join us?" That was more like it. The way I was used to Soupy asking to get something done.

"Sure," I said. I didn't feel like staying in the room anymore. I decided to butt my smoke out.

Zone 4 was where we kept all the heavy-duty stuff—engine exhaust systems, batteries, tires, hoses, rope and electrical cable in bulk rolls, barrels of Varsol and chemicals. Zone 4 was as big as Zones 1, 2 and 3 put together. I wandered up and down until I caught the trail of Stinky Bob at an intersection of two aisles. Turned left and the smell got worse. Getting closer. I found him behind a low wall of Quaker State 80-weight gear oil. He was sitting on a five-gallon pail of Lemon Gojo Hand Cleaner, reading a grocery-store tabloid. Picture of an alien shaking Jimmy Carter's hand on the cover. "Hey Bob," I said.

"Hi Walter," he said, hardly looking up. He was heavy, short grey hair, in his forties. He was like my dad but his voice was soft. No matter how bad he smelled, he always seemed neat and clean in the morning—laundered green-denim work shirt and pants, clean-shaven, good fingernails.

"Bob—Mr. Campbell wants you in the coffee room. All of us are there. I think he's got some kind of announcement."

Stinky Bob folded the paper and hefted himself up. He was barely taller standing than sitting. When he got up he pushed his smell towards me. Like just the act of moving generated some sort of reaction with the atmosphere. Danny would say it wasn't just the smell—Stinky Bob was a total sensory experience. And Danny knew, because he had to work with him most. You could almost see it, like a cloud drifting from him, with hot spots at his crotch, his armpits. Until the full force hit you, then it was bright lights. You could feel it touch you. At first gradually, like a wet hand brushing you in the dark, making goose bumps pop on your arms. Then it would punch you hard, a jab of stink in the gut. And I swear, you could taste it, a garlic burn on the end of your tongue. Unless you were unlucky enough to gulp a big breath, when it sat in the back of your mouth like a rotten egg. Stinky Bob.

Bob ran both his hands through his brush cut. The smell of sweat released from his armpits—whew! I nearly staggered, choked back a gag, pretended to cough. "I suppose it's either raises or pink slips," Stinky Bob said. Punctuated his joke with a burp.

I retreated, turned down the aisle, getting a head-start to outrun Bob. "Sure. Whatever," I said over my shoulder. "I guess it's serious."

Back at the coffee room nobody was saying much. When Soupy was around, he had a way of killing conversation, unless

31

he was doing the talking. Soupy was sucking on his cigarette—my cigarette—like his life depended on it. Squatting on his heels, alone against the wall. The rest of us—twenty-five or thirty or so—sitting around the tables or slouched against the opposite wall. I ducked over and leaned against the Coke machine. Stinky Bob was a ways behind. In a minute or so, he stood at the door. He was huffing and puffing. Soupy stood up, said, "Bob, please join us."

Stinky Bob shuffled a little, tilted in the doorway until the exhaust fan caught a whiff of him and sucked it into the room. I think everybody in the room, except maybe Tattoo Terri, was holding their breath. He moved back a bit, mumbled, "If it's all right with you, Mr. Campbell, I'll just stand out here." There was an audible sound as everybody let go a lungful of air at the same time.

Soupy kept it up: "I insist, Bob. We're all family here. We're on the same team. When I say 'pull' we need to pull *together*. I want all of us to hear what I have to say, and to share our feelings." Stinky Bob shuffled a little more, took a half-step. His eyes darted to and fro, trying to figure our reactions. Rose with the Nose, the receptionist, let out a groan, and Stinky Bob hesitated. My nose wrinkled involuntarily as his smell wafted in.

It was Tattoo Terri who spoke up. "Look Max"—she was the only one who ever bothered to call Mr. Campbell "Max" and not "Mr. Campbell," even though he knocked himself out trying to get us to—"Look Max," she said, "let's be realistic here. Let's face this challenge and find a solution where we all can feel good. You know, win-win, all green lights, no blocking." Tattoo Terri was using the lingo she'd picked up at the team-building work-shop the week before, when Soupy had brought some guy in to teach us all to be our own managers. Soupy nodded. He sucked this stuff up like a sponge. Terri went on: "Bob isn't comfortable coming in to join us. He's just trying to be sensitive to our needs. Right Bob?" Bob looked a little lost—he'd skipped the work-shop. He probably couldn't figure out what she was talking about. Hell, I was there and I was having trouble following it. But he took his cue from Tattoo Terri and nodded. She contin-ued: "And some of the others have expressed their needs." Terri looked hard at Rose with the Nose. "That is, if you consider a grunt or a groan an expression, from someone who is obviously so fucking insensitive to others." Soupy shook his head, and looked like he was trying to figure out what to say. Rose with the Nose rolled her eyes. Tattoo Terri ground out her cigarette—my cigarette—and finished: "Why not let Bob listen outside?"

Soupy was all fidgety-like again. Cleared his throat, said, "Yes, well Terri, aside from the hostility, I guess you've articu-lated one position." He blew out so his cheeks puffed up. He was pale, except for a big red blotch on his forehead and another on his neck. "I don't want hostility. Christ, not now." Talking to himself.

Stinky Bob had already backed out the door. "I'll stay out here, Mr. Campbell."

"Well sure, I guess if you're comfortable with that—"

"In fact," Bob said, "I'll just go over to the loading dock and listen to you all on the intercom."

"You can do that?" Soupy looked around.

"With the phone," Tattoo Terri said. "This phone is set so you can access it to listen as an intercom-speaker from another line."

"Right," said Soupy.

"I do it all the time." Stinky Bob was saying. "At coffee time. I mean I usually take coffee by myself, sometimes I like to hear people. Talking and stuff." His own voice trailed off as he moved away.

Soupy was having trouble with his smoke—my smoke. He'd already dropped it about three times, and finally crushed it with the toe of his shoe. He stared at the door after Bob, rubbed his palms together. The red blotch on his forehead had grown all the way back into his hairline. Suddenly Bob's voice squeaked out from the speaker on the telephone on the wall behind Soupy. "Hi," Bob said, and we all jumped.

"You can hear me all right?" Soupy said, stooping over a bit to speak at the phone.

"Loud and clear like always," Bob said. "You don't even have to stand that close. I can hear all the way across the room just fine." I think all of us were racking our brains, trying to remember what we'd ever said to regret. Wondering if Stinky Bob had been listening. Lots of times Danny and I trashed everybody. Rose's nose, Terri's tattoos, Soupy's bowties. Bob's smell.

Finally, Soupy came out and told us that Danny was dead. I'll say this much for Soupy. He kept it simple for once. "I've got a tragic, unfortunate announcement. Daniel Weybourne died last night. In a car accident. Let us all take a few minutes to remember him. I'll let everyone know details of the service as they become available. Let us remember him." He left it at that. No speeches. No sermons. Soupy turned to face the wall. Bowed his head. Rubbed his face. I moved to the table and sat down, pulled out my smokes and gave one to Tattoo Terri without her asking.

She cleared her throat and I thought she might say something. But she didn't.

About half the room started bawling. Rose with the Nose led the chorus. At first I thought the air conditioning had gone on the blink, a bad bearing or something. She was screeching really high but not too loud, with a kind of *ka-chunk* when she breathed in. I didn't join in. I didn't know enough to cry when I had the chance, back then.

Tattoo Terri didn't cry either. Not quite. I found myself staring at her, and she stared back. I could see tears welling up, how green her eyes were. Usually when I looked at her I just saw tattoos, but this time I saw her eyes. She broke off the stare. She ran her hand under her smock and rubbed her neck, barely moving the shirt collar enough to show a wing of butterfly over her collarbone. "Rose," she called out. It was the first thing anybody had said. "Rose, cut it out." Rose kept at it. "Rose!" Tattoo Terri was almost yelling. The cords on her neck stuck out.

"Terri," someone said. A small voice, coming from the speaker on the phone. Stinky Bob. "Terri," Bob said. "Calm down. Be cool. Don't do anything you'll regret."

Terri jumped up, knocked the chair over. Grabbed the handset, screamed into the mouthpiece. "Shut up, Bob. He's dead, Bob. Shut the fuck up." Slammed the phone down, stormed out. She took her cigarette—my cigarette—with her. Technically, she could have been fired for that. Smoking in the warehouse outside the coffee room.

Bob's voice came out of the speaker. "Good-bye." A click.

We had to go back to work. We couldn't stop working because Danny was dead. There were orders to fill, stock to be inventoried, deliveries to be dispatched. Cars and trucks kept breaking down out there, mechanics in garages phoned for parts, and we shipped 'em out. I spent the morning unloading trailers with Tattoo Terri. It was a job that I would usually do with Danny, or that Danny would do with Stinky Bob. Danny always drove the forklift. The forklift was Danny's baby. He had even installed an 8-track. Liked to play Led Zep tapes or BTO. Strung a row of dingle balls along the roll cage, stuck a chipped plaster statue of the Virgin Mary to the dashboard with a knot of duct tape. That was Danny. He wasn't even Catholic.

I let Tattoo Terri take the forklift. She just got on and started off-loading pallets and I didn't try to stop her. She was a good lift operator. We kept working right through coffee, Terri driving and me swamping, breaking down the loads, stacking loose crates on skids, arranging the stock by zone, double-checking the counts the receiver had signed for. Hardly said six words to each other, except maybe "This one," or "Move that there." No tunes.

I was busting a nut and sweating hard, even though it was cool in the trailers, November and all. I snuck a quick sniff under my arm for B.O. thinking Terri was out on the dock. But she had got down from the lift and was right behind me. "He's got some kind of problem with his glands," she said.

Startled, embarrassed, I spun around. "Huh? No, I was just—" What was I just doing? How do you say that?

"Bob," Terri said. "He's got something with his glands or organs. It's natural, he can't help it."

"Oh." I didn't know what else to say. I was thinking I didn't smell too bad.

We knocked off at five minutes to noon, made for the time clock. Most times at lunch, Danny and I would head across the street to the Dairy Queen. He'd grab a burger, fries and a shake. I'd eat the sandwiches my mom packed for me in waxed paper. We'd talk hockey, cars, music, girls. Maybe I'd pick up a banana split for dessert. Other times I'd just stay in the warehouse at lunch, read westerns or do crosswords. I liked the ones where you solved puzzles. Acrostics.

Stinky Bob and Tattoo Terri went up the road to the Ti-Jaune Tavern lunchtime every day and I asked if I could go along. I didn't much feel like going across the street by myself and didn't want to hang around the warehouse either. The noon buzzer sounded and Terri clocked both her and Bob's cards. "Hustle your ass, Walter," she said, "we only got a half an hour." I punched out and chased after her. Bob had ducked out early to fire up his rusted Datsun and was waiting at the door. Terri dove in the front and pulled the bucket forward and I scrambled in. Stinky Bob popped the clutch and we were moving before the door was closed. I got a noseful of the inside of the car and tried to hold my breath. It was like being inside a hockey sock that had never been washed.

Terri hit the On button for the radio. A Bee Gees song. Over the music she called "Fag!" and stuck her hand between the front seats. At first I thought she meant Andy Gibb, then it registered. I figured what the hell and dished a cigarette out, stuck it between her fingers. It was the rose hand. Maybe the smoke would cut through Stinky Bob's smell. The back window wouldn't open. About ten pine trees dangled from the rearview.

A five-minute ride—one light up 49th and across the tracks—

Stinky Bob drove in less than three. Pulled up in the fire lane right outside the tavern entrance, just under the sign that said "No Parking—Towaway 24 Hours." Tattoo Terri had the door open before the car lurched to a stop and so did Stinky Bob. I fiddled to find the lever that moved the seat forward. "Hey, I forgot my lunch," I said. "Too bad," Terri said. "Barley sandwiches for Walter," Bob said. "Don't bother to lock it."

At that time, I hadn't been in too many beer parlours, and the Ti-Jaune looked like all the rest. Round tables with terry-cloth covers, battered chrome and vinyl chairs, jukebox, cigarette machine, pool table. Just as we sat down, a waitress plunked twelve glasses of draft beer on the table. "I think we'll be needing another dozen, Mitzi," Stinky Bob said, and drank one down in a gulp.

"Work up a thirst, eh," Mitzi said. She balanced her empty tray on her hip.

"Remembering the dead," Bob answered, picking up another. Tattoo Terri raised a glass and tilted it towards Bob. "To Danny," she said. She glanced sideways at me and gave a little nod. I grabbed a beer too and sipped.

Mitzi shifted her weight again. "Five-forty." Tattoo Terri and Stinky Bob drank. I fumbled in my pocket. Pulled out two twos, two fives. "Your round," Terri said. I gave Mitzi seven. She shuffled four quarters from the change dispenser at her waist and slapped them on the table. Kept the other sixty cents for a tip without me telling her to. Terri and Bob were into their third beers and I was barely finished my first when Mitzi brought the next round. Terri opened her bag, counted out five ones, picked up a couple of quarters from the table. "Keep the change," she said.

"Yeah right," Mitzi said. Folded the bills in half along the long edge, added them to a bunch already woven through her fingers. I looked at the clock. Already ten after twelve. "How we gonna drink all these?" I asked.

"With great haste," Stinky Bob said, and drained another glass. "Hurry up," he said.

"I gotta go talk to Steve," Tattoo Terri said. She got up and took two fresh beers with her. Walked over to the pool table, talked to some guy. Biker type, black leather vest, black T, big wallet chained to his jeans dragging halfway down his ass. He gave Terri a cigarette, she gave him a beer.

"Here's to Danny," I said. Toasted with Bob and drank the beer down in a swallow. Bob did the same. Mine backwashed a bit into my nose. Terri came and took the last quarters from the table. "Any requests?" she said. She went to the jukebox. The Stones, "Dead Flowers."

We'd never really had a conversation in the year I'd worked at the warehouse, so Stinky Bob and I sat without saying much. We watched guys shoot pool. Watched the television where a soap opera played without sound. Watched the hand on the clock sweep through the seconds over the cooler behind the bar. The clock's face plastered with the logo of a beer that they didn't make anymore. Watched Tattoo Terri move through the room. Talking to one, then another of the regulars. For about the thousandth time I wondered how many different tattoos she had, where they might be. I'd seen a half a dozen—the roses, the parrot, the butterfly, a mushroom on her shoulder, a vine around her ankle. What designs were on her breasts? Her back? Her butt? What might be engraved on the inside of her thighs, in the well of her navel?

Stinky Bob hunched forward and drew me into the thick of his smell. He belched and the release of recently-consumed beer gases was refreshing. "Twenty-seven," he said.

"Huh?" I said.

"Terri," he said. "Twenty-seven tattoos."

At first I wanted to ask him how he knew what I was thinking. Asked instead, "How do you know?" Bob didn't answer, sucked another glass of draft. I persisted: "I mean, did you count them or something?" I could've kicked myself. I couldn't lose the image of Stinky Bob in his green work shirt, counting tattoos on Terri's naked body.

Stinky Bob licked his upper lip real slow. I had an attack of the willies. I could feel the beer working on my empty stomach. Heat flushed my face. My trousers felt like they were full of pink fibreglass insulation. I squirmed. "What do you suppose?" he asked. The smell from Bob nauseated me. Each word oozed, dropped from his mouth like a fish flopping on the bottom of a boat. Flopping and bleeding and dying. Stinking. But it was me whose mouth moved like a fish. Opening and closing, no words.

Stinky Bob laughed. A single "Hah!" full of beery bad breath. He dunked his fingers in a glass and flicked drops of beer in my face. "Snap out if it, Walter. Should I call a doctor?" Laughed again. "I didn't count any of Terri's tattoos. I asked her, same as you would." I probably looked like I'd just eaten a hot pepper. Sweat beaded on my forehead. My eyes burned. I shook my head a little bit. Bob repeated, "I asked her, Walter. I asked Terri how many tattoos." He went into a fit of laughing. Kind of a bark at the back of his throat, with a snort each time he breathed.

It broke down into a series of sneezes. His laugh smelled like compost.

I started to laugh along. The kind of half-laugh where you don't really get the joke. I had to think about turning the corners of my mouth up. I hoisted a beer and drank. Tried to take it all in one pull. Stinky Bob blew his nose into a blue and white handkerchief, wiped at his eyes. "You're quite something, Walter. Like a spring lamb you are." He looked into his handkerchief, examined what was there. "Now Danny," he went on. "He might have known more about those tattoos." I coughed beer back into my glass and up my nose. Bob looked at me, grinning. "Of course if he did, he took his secrets with him. Eh, Wally?" I drank another beer, lit up a smoke. I hated it when anyone called me Wally.

Tattoo Terri came back to the table and slid into her chair. "You guys look like you were having a time." She reached for my cigarettes on the table. I covered her hand. "No," I said. "No, no, no. For once buy your own goddamned smokes. I'm sick and tired of you mooching off me. Listening to 'Walter can you bum me a fag,' like I'm some queer. Get your own fucking fags."

Tattoo Terri pulled her hand from under mine. Held it close to her, like I'd hurt her or something, which I hadn't. Then she relaxed. Regained her cool as always. "A little testy, are we?" Her voice was smooth as ice cream. She was mad, I could tell. The three of us looked at different things. Not each other. We waited in silence. Drank the last of the round.

"Aw shit," I said finally. "Have a cigarette. I hate it when a girl sulks." I tossed the deck over to her. "Have the whole damn package. I quit."

Terri drew a smoke from the box, tapped it on her thumbnail a couple of times to tamp it. Stinky Bob waved Mitzi to bring more beer. "I'm hardly a girl, Walter. And I certainly never sulk," Terri said. But she was smiling and I did too. Flipped her Zippo open and lit the cigarette. Handed the rest back to me.

"No," I said. "Keep 'em. I quit. This is my last one." I blew a stream of smoke to a ceiling fan going around and around above my head.

"Really," Tattoo Terri said. "You quit. Just like that."

"Sure. Just like that. For Danny. Like a tribute to Danny. He hated smoking. I mean, he smoked like a chimney, but he was always trying to quit." I felt kind of stupid saying this. But proud at the same time. I had a sudden urge to talk, to say anything about Danny. "You know," I said. "Danny had nicknames for all you guys." Stinky Bob drank. Tattoo Terri shrugged, took the pack of cigarettes and put them in her bag. "He did," I went on. "For everybody. Rose with the Nose. Soupy Campbell. Fat Pat. Attilla the Hank." I took the last drag off the last cigarette I would ever smoke. Dropped the butt in an empty glass.

I looked at Terri. She looked back. "He called you Tattoo Terri. I mean, I guess, sure. What else would he call you, right?" I nodded to Bob. "And, well. He called you Stinky Bob. No offence. He just called you that. A nickname." The two of them were smiling. Bob looked at the beer in his hand. Terri looked over at the pool table.

Bob said, "He had a few for you too."

"Me?" I said.

"He called you Wimpy Walter," Terri said. "Or just Wimpy."

"Sometimes Wild Walter," Bob said.

"But usually Weird Wally," Terri finished. Mitzi brought a dozen more beers. Bob paid, tipped her two bucks. It was twenty-six minutes after noon. "We'll be late today," Terri said.

"To Danny," Bob said. "Dead Danny."

"Dead Danny," Terri said, raising a glass.

"Dead Danny," I said. We all drank.

Industrial Accidents

Four men sit in the lunchroom of a chemical plant.

Andy has a pen in each hand. He is doing two crosswords at once. The newspaper he reads has two sets of clues for the same puzzle. With the right hand, blue ink, he answers the cryptic clues in the bottom right corners of the blanks. With the left, red, he answers the quick clues in the top left. He hopes one day to complete both simultaneously.

Meanwhile, Jason struggles with a different puzzle in the tabloid daily. He asks, "What's a six-letter word for pan-liner, starts with a T?" His grime-etched fingers are knotted around a pencil he's sharpened with his knife.

Asleep on a chair in the corner, Bruce makes a sound in his throat, not quite a snore.

With a pocket screwdriver, Ditmar scrapes the leavings from

his pipe onto the lunchroom table. He breaks up the cold dottle, separating the ash from bits of tobacco that are merely scorched. He brushes the ash to the floor, then scoots the rest into his tobacco pouch.

"Teflon," Andy says without looking up. Three puzzles at once, he thinks.

"Teflon," Ditmar repeats. "Teflon is a killer."

Jason puts the pencil behind his ear, opens his paper to the page with the photo of the bikini-clad Beauty Of The Day. Teflon thighs, he thinks. He uses an Exacto knife to cut out the picture. He folds it carefully, minding where the creases are, and tucks it into the breast pocket of his coveralls. Later, at the end of shift, he will add it to the stack of pictures in his locker clipped from the last two years' of papers.

"It's true," Ditmar continues. "Researchers at a chemical factory very much like this one. Trying to make a synthetic lubricant. They mixed some formula, it didn't work." Ditmar checks his watch.

"Really," Jason says. Andy scribbles on newsprint.

Bruce dreams of trout.

Ditmar pinches a clump of tobacco into the bowl of his pipe. "Then they sat down to lunch, just as we are doing now." A thin chain tethers a cigarette lighter to the leg of the lunchroom table. Ditmar pulls it towards him and clicks the flame to life. How sad, he thinks, as he does each time: a pipe should be lit with a wooden match. Regulations prevent him and all workers from bringing personal matches or lighters into the plant. "But one of them left it on the burner. A terrible oversight, or perhaps brilliant."

"Really," Jason says. He runs the Exacto blade under a thumbnail.

"Truly," Ditmar says. "The stuff brewed and bubbled while they ate." The tar in the stem of his pipe gurgles as he puffs. "The fumes killed them, every one." He lets the smoke curl from his lips to wash over his face. "When the rescue team found them, it was like a still life, only dead. Sitting at a laboratory bench, sandwiches in hand. And the beaker of solution baked into the famous non-stick coating."

"Really," Jason says.

"Urban myth," Andy says, both a response to Ditmar, and an answer to a clue.

"One of them, they say, was slumped over a crossword puzzle." Ditmar places his pipe in the ashtray chained to the table.

Bruce rouses himself from his slumber. I will paint my boat blue, he thinks.

Noises

She had just finished throwing up when she heard the doorbell. Beverly reached for a hand towel from the built-in linen closet in her mother-in-law's bathroom. The thick textured fabric rubbed roughly against her lips as she wiped her mouth. She ran water in the sink to wash down the bits of regurgitated grapefruit pith, toast and mucous, then rinsed the cloth and held it to her forehead. Her post-puke fog left her enervated yet relieved. The tension in her neck and shoulders had eased, the sour wedge in her gut had disappeared. Morning sickness— morning, noon and night. She felt best those few minutes right after vomiting.

The doorbell rang.

Beverly caught a glimpse of herself in the mirror over the sink, and was surprised at the reflection. Despite nausea, she looked good. Everyone said, you absolutely glow. Her short brown hair, although dishevelled, shone with a hint of a wave and body it hadn't had before. Her complexion was clear and silky. Colour flashed on her cheeks. She looked terrific, but felt like shit. Six-and-a-half more months of this?

The doorbell rang.

She brushed her teeth. She was careful not to probe too deeply with the brush—that provoked a gag reaction. The roof of her mouth and the back of her throat felt like they were coated with a thick paste, and she suddenly retched—just once, bringing nothing up—thinking of wet papier-mâché.

The doorbell rang.

"Hold your horses or go away," she muttered as she went downstairs.

The visitor stood close to the townhouse, inside the drip line of the eave. He was reaching to ring the bell again when Beverly opened the door. She said nothing, just looked at him through the screen. The rain had plastered his thinning white hair to his scalp. A few drops hung in his bushy brows. His skin was very pale. He looked fifty, maybe sixty years old. Beverly thought of a potato, and with his blue eyes swimming in his face, decided he should be Irish.

"Mary and Frank aren't in," the man said, nodding his head towards the front door of the neighbouring condominium, ten feet away. A pair of hedge clippers, red wooden handles opened like an X, and a long-handled spade were on the patch of grass that passed for lawn beside the shared sidewalk. The morning's downpour had slackened to a drizzle, and the tools seemed varnished by wet. Beverly remembered the poem she had read in college about a wheelbarrow. So much depends.

She didn't speak.

"Mary and Frank aren't home," he started again. "I sometimes go there for lunch when the weather's bad." He reached a hand inside his windbreaker—an old-fashioned one, Beverly noticed, probably rayon, collarless with frayed corduroy trim and a dulled brass zipper—and he pulled out a wrinkled brown paper sack. The shoulders of his jacket were dark with rain, even his lunch bag looked damp. "They let me use their microwave. For my lunch."

Somewhere in the neighbourhood, a beep-beep-beep signalled that a truck was backing up, then it stopped. Beverly stared through the mesh of the screen, looking at a point over the man's left shoulder, as if she were doing sums in her head. Finally, she said, "I don't know why you're telling me this."

The man sidled over to invade her gaze, and looked at her with a real in-the-eye look. He smiled. "I thought I'd see if Gladys was in. She sometimes comes over when I eat with Mary and Frank." There was a quaver in his voice, as if he were trying to prevent his teeth from chattering. He shrugged. "But I guess she's not home either."

"Gladys," Beverly said. For a second she didn't know who he was talking about, then it clicked. Nobody called her Gladys. She was Gaddie. Her mother-in-law, Colm's mother. They were house-sitting for Gaddie while she spent six months in Africa with Christian Helpmates International.

The man's khaki pants were faded to a gloss, his work boots scuffed and cracking. One steel toecap poked through a hole in the leather. She glanced at the spade and clippers. Had Gaddie said anything about the gardener? Beverly couldn't remember— really, she had stopped paying attention to the woman. She and Colm had settled in only a week ago. It was Gaddie's idea, cooked up when she found out Beverly was expecting. After all, she had said, Beverly and Colm were starting their family late, starting everything late ("Most of my friends had four or five babies by the time they were your age!"). They had all those student loans, had spent all that time in school and travelling everywhere, living in apartments. If they stayed until the baby came, paid off their debts, maybe they could save the down payment for a house of their own. Besides, someone had to look after the condo.

So they sold or gave away most of the things that they had acquired over the years as cast-offs or in garage sales, and moved in. The few good pieces of furniture were packed into Gaddie's garage. Colm insisted on keeping his boxes of engineering textbooks. Beverly wouldn't part with her bolts of fabric and rolling racks of clothes she had made. They kept a steamer trunk full of vinyl records because they didn't have the time to sort through and separate Peter Frampton from Bob Dylan, then argue over what to keep and what to trash. Colm's 1969 BSA Lightning motorcycle was scattered in several pieces. Gaddie had tut-tutted: "Where will you park my car?"

"There's room outside on the apron," Colm replied.

Before she boarded her plane to Washington, D.C., where the Christians were assembling for the assault on the dark continent, the three of them had spent two days in the townhouse. Gaddie had fussed non-stop.

By the phone in the kitchen she assembled a thick three-ring binder with a green cover, sectioned with stiff-tabbed dividers. She compiled phone lists of neighbours, missionary contacts, emergency numbers for fire, flood, pestilence and war. An itinerary of her African trip, complete with brochures about the places she would visit. Operations and maintenance instructions for the washer and dryer, fridge and stove, convection oven, microwave, freezer, televisions, stereos, the furnace. Insurance policies. Lots of insurance policies—the widow of the owner of an insurance agency believed in good coverage.

Gaddie talked her way through those two days. "That's Mr. Gilford," she would say as a car pulled into the little lane that wound through the units in her part of the complex. "He's chair of the Risk Management Committee. You'll need to call him if the roof leaks or a tree falls against the house." "There's Betty Peel, Snow Removal Task Force," she said, pointing out an elderly woman power-walking in the early morning. "Don't hesitate to call her in a blizzard." (To offer assistance or demand service? Gaddie didn't say.) About a silver-haired man who walked his poodle through the green commons twice a day: "Wife left two years ago." Three women in saris, pushing a shopping cart from the supermarket down the road: "Never so much as a hello to us, just nattering away to themselves in their own gibberish." Two clean-cut men riding matching bicycles, one with a white helmet, the other yellow: "Those two are gay! I know because they told me themselves, they tell everybody." A young mother limping after her two boys as they kick a soccer ball through the parking lot: "Recovering from hip replacement." A man who drove a panel van with the logo of a painting and decorating company: "Jewish." A woman with her hair in curlers: "Alcoholic." Beverly remembered Mary and Frank: "Daughter joined a cult."

Beverly looked at the man again. His shoulders seemed

hunched a little more, his shivering intensified, the look in his eyes now plainly miserable. She noticed a clump of wet clay on the blade of the spade. In her own little patio at the back, Gaddie had taken up all the annuals before she left, deadheaded the perennials, pruned and mulched the planters, and generally made the little garden fallow. She said she wouldn't dream of foisting her chores on them, especially with Beverly in her condition. The meaning was clear—she didn't trust them to do it to her standards. Beverly couldn't remember if Gaddie had mentioned the gardener for the common areas of the complex.

It seemed Gaddie had exhausted in detail all the routines of the complex: trash collection on Tuesdays now, but the schedule slips a day after every statutory holiday, so by the time she gets back, it'll be back to Tuesdays. Put the cans *by* the lane, not *in* the lane. Separate the paper and metal and glass. No visitor parking except in the designated lot, absolutely no stopping in fire lanes, use of the picnic pagoda by appointment only, 10:30 outside noise curfew.

A drop of water clung to the tip of the man's nose. Beverly suddenly thought, This man is cold and wet and hungry. "What the hell," she said, "Come on in."

In the tiny vestibule, the man struggled with the laces on his boots. A toe showed through one sock. He slipped off his jacket, and held it in one hand slightly away from himself, reached for a hanger in the open front closet, and swept his eyes over the contents—Colm's leather bomber, Beverly's raw silk quilted jacket, Gaddie's lambswool overcoat zipped in a plastic garment bag. Colm's ancient golf clubs that had belonged to his father. He turned and hung the jacket on the doorknob, where it dripped onto the ceramic tiles.

Beverly led the man through the hall and up the half-flight of stairs to the kitchen. The townhouse was tall and narrow, the third unit in a building of four; that building in turn one of twenty-five or so arrayed on the condominium property. Each unit was a five-level split, the levels staggered front to back to maximize the use of space. The single-car garage occupied most of the main level, with the front entrance and matchbook lawn. On the second level, the kitchen and family room opened through a sliding glass door onto the compact patio.

Beverly had set up a long folding table in the middle of the family room, and piled it high with fabric, half-finished garments, and her sewing machine. She kept the long vertical blinds closed over the glass door, to shut out the patio and its orderliness. Interlocking colour-coordinated paving stones, scrubbed and swept. The rigid planters terraced in every nook and cranny. The barbecue with its insulated cover, covered again by a plastic sheet. *Une place pour chaque chose et chaque chose à sa place.* She had detested high school French.

The man plunked his sodden paper sack on the counter between the two rooms. "Nice place," he said. He walked over and looked out between the slats of the blinds. "Neat yard," he said. "Very nice indeed."

Beverly stood by the stairs, watching as he moved through the space. His shivering seemed to have subsided. He ran a hand through the strands of his hair, then looked at his palm slick with the rain. "I'll get a towel," Beverly said. When she returned, the man was standing by the sound system console next to the fireplace. She watched as he ran a finger over the stacks of CDs. He pushed the Eject button and checked the disc that was cued.

"Here's a towel," Beverly said.

"Hmm," the man said. He stayed by the stereo, pushed the CD platter closed, then punched Play. The first couple of bars played, then the voice. Tom Jones. "It's not unusual to be . . ." The man cocked his head like the RCA Victor dog, and adjusted the volume up a couple of notches.

"Please," Beverly said. She moved across the room to pick up the remote control from the worktable and turned off the music. The man shrugged and turned towards her. She flicked her wrist and tossed him the towel. Carefully, he dried his hands, the palms, the backs, between the fingers, wiped his face and brow, then drew it over his hair. He examined the items on the table. "Making clothes?" he said.

"Yes," Beverly replied. "No, not exactly. Costumes." It was an important distinction to her. Gaddie was always calling her a seamstress. "For a children's theatre." She moved so the table was between them. "That's what I do. I sew costumes for theatre. Actually, I design and sew costumes. I'm making a mermaid costume."

"Very admirable," he replied. The man looked at her sewing machine. "Pfaff. Beautiful," he said. He kept his eyes on the machine as he handed the used towel to Beverly. She snatched it.

"What about your lunch," she said. She folded the towel in her hands. "The microwave's by the sink."

He smiled, showing teeth brilliantly white and even. "Right," he said. "To lunch." He went to the kitchen, rummaged in his paper sack and pulled out an old margarine container.

Beverly sat at the worktable. She realized she was still kneading the towel, and let it drop to the carpet. She picked up the piece of cloth she had been working with. The play's director had asked for flesh-coloured spandex. Whose flesh, she wondered. Not this man's chalky flesh. Not the coffee-brown of the clerk at the fabric store where she had purchased it. She had tried to describe what she was looking for, tried not to describe it in terms of skin; finally the clerk had exclaimed, Oh by all means, we have lots of flesh-tone. Like flesh-coloured crayons, or the colour of dolls, not really the true colour of anyone's flesh, but a colour that suggested a certain kind of flesh. She wished she hadn't told him what she was doing. Very admirable, what was that supposed to mean?

Beverly made a few practice seams, working with scraps of fabric before she started to cut the pattern. A bodysuit for a mermaid's costume. She had finally settled for a blend of cotton-poly reinforced with Lycra. She needed it ready for a fitting tomorrow. She fingered the shiny remnant, stretched it between her hands, and watched the man.

He put the food in the microwave, then stood, examining the panel. "How does this—" he said. She cut in on his question: "Hit Reheat, then enter a time, then hit Start."

The appliance beeped, then whirred to life as he operated the controls. "These things are all a little different," he said. He kept his back turned to her, staring through the little window as his food rotated on the platter. The aroma of canned beef stew filled the room. Beverly thought she could smell the salt, the fat, imagined the congealed gravy turning soft and corn-starch slippery. Her gorge rose. She bolted from her chair and ran up the three flights of stairs to the master bathroom. She dry-heaved. When she thought it was over, a vision of the worn plastic tub of stew popped into her head, and she had another round of spasms. Her throat was raw and constricted, as if she had swallowed hot stones.

Beverly sponged her face, then almost lost it again as she scooped a handful of water from the faucet to rinse her mouth. Her stomach muscles and diaphragm were cramping from the days upon days of morning sickness. In the mirror, she saw not exactly a stranger, but a different self. She spoke out loud and watched her mouth as it moved, as if she were reading her own lips: "What the hell is that man doing in my kitchen?" She grabbed the cordless phone from the bedroom and started down. Stopping on the stairs a couple of steps above the kitchen level, she crossed her arms to keep her hands from shaking. "You have to leave," she said.

The man stood at the counter, shoveling stew into his mouth with one hand; with the other he poked around in her cupboard. He looked at Beverly, the phone. "Can I take the spoon? I found it in a drawer," he said.

"Take the spoon, I don't care. You have to go. Now." The man licked the spoon, stuck it in his shirt pocket. He popped the lid onto the container, opened his mouth like he was going to speak, then closed it. She didn't follow him to the door, only listened to the rustle as he donned his boots and jacket.

"I'll leave it in the mailbox," he called up to her.

"Just go," she said. "Get out." She wasn't sure her voice was loud enough to be heard.

"The spoon," he said. She heard the door open and close,

waited for the sound of the screen door latching. She peeked around the corner, then hurried to the door and shot the bolt. She put her eye to the peephole. He was just a few steps from her, exactly where he had been standing when he rang the doorbell. He held the container under his chin, and spooned food into his mouth. He was looking at the door, at her. Beverly's hand trembled as she slid the burglar chain into place, careful not to make a noise.

A rush of blood throbbed in her temples. She panted in short breaths, too fast and too shallow, until she started to feel faint. Hyperventilating. She knew the remedy: breathe into a bag. She tiptoed back to the kitchen, ignored the crumpled paper sack the man had left on the counter, and found another in a drawer. She cupped it around her face and concentrated on each inhalation and exhalation. She twitched when the phone began to howl with an off-the-hook alarm. She found it on the couch in the family room and pressed the Talk button to disconnect. She slid to the floor and buried herself in the bag. The crinkle of kraft paper marked the rhythm of her breathing.

When she looked through the peephole again, the man was gone. The spade and clippers still lay on the grass. She didn't open the door to check the mailbox.

■   ■   ■

That evening, Colm made a sandwich for his supper. Ham and cheese, a bagel from the freezer. He zapped it in the microwave to thaw, halved it, then toasted and buttered it, careful to spread the butter evenly to the edges. He peeled the outer layers from a head of iceberg lettuce, tossing out those that were the least bit spotted with brown. "You're sure you don't want one?" he asked. "You have to eat something."

"Oh god, don't even mention food." Beverly spoke around a mouthful of pins pressed between her lips. She had sketched a pattern for the mermaid suit on onionskin paper and laid it on the floor. She knelt down and pinned the fabric in place. Quiet jazz drifted from a Toots Thielman CD, turned low.

"You need to eat. You can't expect to stay healthy if you don't eat and then throw up all day. You or the baby."

"I'll have some cheese and crackers."

"Cheese and crackers! For supper?" Colm spread a thick layer of mustard on one of the bagel halves. He was slightly disgusted by the bright yellow goop from the no-name jar. He had scoured his mother's fridge, cupboards, and pantry shelf in the basement, hoping to find good mustard, but to no avail. He added Dijon mustard to the list he was keeping in his head, essentials that Gaddie's house lacked: capers, fresh garlic and ginger, prosciutto, kalamata olives, feta and chèvre, sesame oil, fish sauce, three-ply toilet paper, citrus-oil household cleaner, decent candles — he couldn't believe that he'd let Beverly and his mother talk him into giving all that stuff away. He'd had a good Dijon, and a fine Russian mustard dressing too, but they hadn't kept any food when they moved. Nothing. The only time Beverly and Gaddie had ever agreed on anything. He was looking forward to shopping on Saturday.

"You need something more substantial than cheese and crackers."

"Melba toast and cheese," Beverly said.

"Green vegetables," Colm said. "The foetus needs folates or it'll be a spina bifida baby." He'd been studying pregnancy, nutrition and prenatal health. I'll do the theory, he said to Beverly, you do the practice. He put the lid on his sandwich and admired his handiwork. He found a box of melba toast and sliced several pieces of cheddar. "How about some broccoli?"

"Ugh. I can't stand the sight of it. Don't even say the word. Just visualizing how it's spelled makes me sick. Yech." Beverly stuck the last of her unused pins into a pincushion. "Is there any celery? Or pickles? It's such a cliché, but I'd kill for pickles."

"Cravings for salty and acidy foods are completely normal." Colm arranged the melba toast and cheese on a plate, four stalks of celery and one of his mother's huge home-made dills and some of her bread and butter pickles too. He brought Beverly's snacks and his sandwich into the family room, and they settled onto the couch. "You didn't get far," he said, looking at the work spread on the carpet. "You said you'd be finished this afternoon."

"I got distracted," Beverly said. She nibbled at a pickle. "A man came to the door."

"Hmm," Colm said as he chewed a mouthful of ham and cheese. He swallowed and added: "Distracted by a man. I should be concerned." He dabbed at the corners of his mouth with his finger, checking for mustard.

She crunched a bite of celery. "I let him in." Beverly told Colm about the visitor. He listened, still at first, then slowly shaking his head. She kept her tone light and nonchalant, how much like a drowned rat the poor man looked, joking how the smell of his stew made her gag, how she chased him out on account of nausea. She left out the parts about her holding the phone with her thumb poised over the 911 speed-dial, bolting the door, breathing into a paper bag. She chased sweet pickles around the plate in her lap with a spear of melba toast.

Colm held his bagel in both hands, as if poised for another bite.

"I gave him an old spoon," Beverly said. "I told him to leave it in the mailbox, but that he had to eat outside." Colm stared. The sound of Toots bending his harmonica around "Take Five" filled the silence.

Finally Colm said, "Wow. I can't believe you'd let him in." Colm put his sandwich down. "I mean, it's so dangerous. You thought he was the gardener, so you let him in, and gave him a spoon? Shouldn't you have asked for ID or something?"

Beverly glanced at Colm. "Don't give me that."

"What. Give you what? What, exactly, am I giving you?"

"That look. That fucking voice. I can practically see the italics when you speak to me like that, your holier-than-thou voice. You suck at sarcasm. The poor bastard was soaking wet."

Colm went outside to check the mailbox. The spoon was there. Back inside, he examined it under the bright kitchen light, looking for a clue to its user. "It's not just some old spoon. It's a piece of mother's flatware." He paced in the narrow strip between the mermaid costume and the coffee table.

"At least he gave it back," she said.

Colm stopped in front of Beverly, pointing the utensil at her. "This would be worth three, maybe five dollars to somebody desperate." Beverly turned her head away from him.

"You're awfully worried about Gaddie's flatware. What about me?"

"Well, what about you? Aren't you responsible? How did you know he was a gardener? He could have been anybody. Did you check the book? No, not Beverly, the book's too much like work. That's how these gangs operate."

"Gangs?" Beverly said. "What are you on about now? Who said anything about a gang? You're doing it again, Colm."

"That's what they do." Colm started pacing again. "They send someone in to case the joint."

Beverly rolled her eyes.

"I saw that," Colm continued. "They case the joint. Then they send eight-year-olds through the basement window, or down the chimney. You know how small those Vietnamese are."

"Oh give me a break, eight-year-olds. Besides, he was closer to sixty-eight," Beverly said. She tossed her plate aside and a pickle fell on the floor. "And who said anything about Vietnamese?"

"Well, was he?"

"Was he what?"

"Vietnamese?"

"He was white. He was a pasty-white, wet old man. White like a boiled potato. If he was anything, he was Irish, as if that matters."

"White?" Colm pounced on the information. "Like a potato. Didn't you think it odd that a gardener would be white like a potato in October? He's been out in the sun all summer, gardening, getting whiter and whiter. Were his hands dirty? Did he have calluses?"

"We didn't shake hands. He had work boots. Worn and dirty work boots," Beverly shot back.

"Jailhouse pallor, that's what he had," Colm said. "The big-house tan." He went into the kitchen, and scrubbed the spoon vigorously with a brush and detergent. "Tuberculosis and hepatitis are rampant in prisons." He scrubbed his hands.

"Oh christ, don't be stupid. You're worse than your mother."

"Don't call me stupid. Or insult my mother. Did I call you stupid? Would she have let some man into her house? I think not."

"Not bloody likely," Beverly said.

"What's that supposed to mean?"

"You think I did something stupid, but you won't say so. So you end up saying really stupid things, Colm. Listen to yourself, for once. Gangs, Vietnamese, 'the big-house tan.' Where do you come up with this stuff?" Beverly rose, picked up her shears off the worktable and squatted down on the floor.

"Did you pick up that pickle?" Colm asked.

"What?"

"You dropped a pickle. Damn," he said, lifting the shiny spoon up to the light.

Beverly hesitated before she cut the fabric. She knelt, back straight, scissors in hand. "Look, he was a nice man. He was wet and cold and needed to warm up his lunch. I let him do that and I threw up and he left. He had a nice smile. Perfect teeth. He said thank you. He returned the spoon. End of story." She scissored deftly down the edge of the pattern.

"White potato skin and perfect teeth. They have free dental care in prisons, you know. Free. They all come out with perfect teeth."

"I'm not listening to this anymore," Beverly said. She found the remote control and hit the button to change the CD to the next platter. The Tragically Hip. She turned up the volume.

"Fine," Colm said. He opened the fridge door and pulled out a can of Guinness Draught. He popped the top and listened as the button of nitrogen gas in the bottom of the can released with a hiss. He took comfort from the knowledge of the engineering that could go into something as simple as a can of beer. He drank a gulp. Nearly as good as the real thing in a Dublin pub. In fact, he liked his beer chilled, even his stout, so maybe better than a Dublin pub. "I'm calling the condo people," he said.

"Go right ahead," Beverly answered. She continued to trim the Lycra, her head bent.

"Fine," Colm said. Tucking the green binder under his arm, and holding the beer and sandwich in either hand, he climbed the three short flights of stairs to the top level.

The upstairs portable handset for the telephone wasn't in its charging cradle, and he got no answer when he used the locator button—the ringer was probably turned off anyway, the battery lasted at least four times as long if you left the ringer off. He sat down on the edge of the bed. He didn't really want to call anyone. He needed to get away from Beverly before he said anything else to regret.

The master bedroom was a large space, with its own five-piece bath accessible through double French doors. He stared at where the ceiling vaulted upward to follow the line of the roof, which was buttressed by two outsized laminated beams. Colm had never been able to determine to his own satisfaction whether the beams were structural elements, or merely for design. Gaddie decorated sparsely here. The walls were a brilliant white. A queen bed with a goose down comforter. An escritoire that had belonged to Colm's grandmother, now used as a dressing table. A simple cushioned chair without arms, draped in a slipcover. A massive white dresser like a slab of marble that she had hired a cabinetmaker to build. The only adornments in the room were an oversized urn filled with impossibly huge dried flowers, a bevelled plate-glass mirror installed on the wall over the dressing table, and a photograph of Colm's father hung dead-centre on the wall above the bed. The expanse of the room seemed like a museum gallery awaiting an installation.

For Beverly, that would mean an installation of laundry, Colm thought. Three of her suitcases sprawled open on the creamy white pile carpet, spilling clothes across the floor. Two half-full laundry baskets had been dropped by the bathroom door. One was for clean things, the other dirty, but Colm never knew which was which. Her shoes were piled in a heap outside the closet. A brassiere hung from the doorknob.

Looking at her clothes, Colm had a sudden rush of panic. It was typical of her to allow a stranger into the house, like a stray cat. She does these things. The Germans probably have a word for it, he thought. Not for her actions, but his panic. Almost-Grief, or Grief-Narrowly-Avoided or the Horror-That-Might-Have-Happened. He would cease to exist without her. It drives him crazy. It makes him say those things, he can't stop himself. Convicts with perfect teeth. Did I actually say that? Colm thought. I don't give a rat's ass about a spoon or gangs.

Colm looked at his father's photograph. A studio portrait, perhaps for an advertisement. Colm guessed that in the photo his father wasn't any older than he was, probably younger. He had a sudden pang of embarrassment—of *course* his father was younger in the photo. Colm was older now than his father had been when he'd died. He felt his ears turn red, and looked about the room, as if he were afraid that someone had heard his thoughts. A son should remember when his father died. Even if he was too young when it happened to remember.

Glum now, he ate the last of his sandwich methodically, drank the beer in rapid sips. It was weird drinking beer here, in this house. He went down to the kitchen, rinsed the plate, put the beer can in the recycling bin. In the family room, he picked up the pickle from near the sofa. He sat down, looked at the pickle, then ate it. He felt something under his leg: the portable phone jammed between two cushions. Loose bits of threads littered the carpet, he could see the glint of straight pins lost in the cut pile. They'll never clean it all up by the time Gaddie comes home.

Beverly worked at the machine now, sewing the seams of the costume. Holding the phone in his hands, he asked: "Are you okay?" Beverly continued her work. "We can get a dog," Colm said. "For when you're alone."

◼   ◼   ◼

Beverly comes to bed late, long after midnight. Colm snores lightly, but wakes when she gags on her toothbrush. She moves into the room, shedding her clothes as she stumbles through the near darkness, leaving a trail of sweater, blouse, bra, slacks and panties, socks. Colm holds open the bedclothes and she slips in naked beside him. Together, they slide their bodies into a familiar nighttime embrace, Beverly on her side, facing away from Colm as he nestles like a spoon behind her. His long lean arm wraps around her and his hand cups the plumpness of her belly below her navel. There is no quickening yet, the round curves of her abdomen do not yet show the changes occurring inside her. Beneath Colm's hand, in Beverly's uterus, cells divide and re-divide, growing and aligning according to their genetic code, with her every breath, her every heartbeat.

"Your bum is cold," Colm says into the nape of her neck.

"You're warm," Beverly answers. "Hug me."

He presses even closer. "You worked late."

"It's done," she says. "One mermaid costume ready for fitting. Except for the seaweed." Colm passes his hand slowly over her stomach, caresses her breast, then glides it across the valley of her waist and up the generous swale of her hip. "That feels nice," Beverly murmurs. His thumb brushes against her pubis. "Mmmm," Beverly responds. He tries to move his fingers between her thighs, gently, but she keeps her knees together. "No," Beverly mumbles. "It's late."

Colm shifts his body, lifts a leg over hers. He nibbles behind her ear. His thumb and forefinger tug at her nipple.

"No Colm. What are you doing."

He lifts himself a little higher, kisses her shoulder. "Please let me in," Colm says. "Please let me in," he says again, his voice now inflected with an Irish lilt. "I'm cold and I'm wet and I'm hungry. I'm just a poor gardener from Limerick who needs a wee bit of comfort."

Beverly tenses. "Stop it, Colm. That's not funny." She grabs his hand and tries to roll away. He begins to kiss her madly on her back as she wriggles. His words are muffled: "Oh, please missus. I'm just a poor man of the soil what needs some warmth and a little solace."

"It's not funny." Beverly pulls away, but Colm tickles her under the ribcage. "Stop. Stop it now." Colm wraps her in a bear hug. She tosses from side to side, jerks back suddenly, catching him in the forehead with her occiput.

"Frisky lass," Colm says, accent now firmly Scots. He presses some of his weight against her. His penis is stiff.

"Shhhh," Beverly whispers, and she stops resisting. "Mmmm," Colm says, but she hushes him again. "No, Colm. I mean it. Listen. Do you hear that?"

"What?"

They lie still. Beverly turns her head and raises it slightly from the pillow. Colm holds her tightly, but quiets. Finally, after a dozen heartbeats, he says, "I don't hear—"

"Shhh," Beverly cuts him off. "There it was again." She pushes his leg away and sits up. "That."

"What?" They both hold their breath.

"That." They both say it at once. Colm sits upright. "Sounded like it was in the kitchen," Beverly whispers. Colm bolts from the bed and scoots in a crouch towards the door. He pulls on a pair of pants he finds on the floor and grabs a stout wooden hanger from the closet. "You stay here," he says, and moves commando-like out of the room.

On the stairs, he looks over his shoulder. Beverly is right behind him. She has slipped on one of his shirts, which covers her almost to her knees. She holds a high-heeled shoe by the toe. "I'm not staying by myself," she says in a whisper. Colm nods.

They make their way down through the levels of the condo to the kitchen, stopping like spooked deer to listen, turning on every light as they go, looking in the bedrooms, the other bathroom, the living and dining areas. The kitchen is empty. Beverly stands where she did at noon, two steps up, clutching her shoe. Colm walks to the sink and puts the hanger down on the counter. "It's just noises. Expansion and contraction of the joists," Colm says. He pours a glass of water from the sink and drinks it off in a draught. Then he looks to where Beverly's work is still scattered.

He goes into the family room to the blinds, and picks up a long wooden dowel that is lying on the carpet. It is usually placed in the door track to block the door closed, to prevent it from being forced open. "Did you take this out?" Colm says.

Beverly stares at the piece of wood. "Wasn't it in the door?" she says. "I haven't been out that door since Gaddie left." Colm pulls the blind back and tries to peer into the night through the reflections on the glass. He checks the latch. "It's locked," he says. He pulls at the door and rocks it, trying to lift it out of the lock.

"That's it," Beverly says. "That's the sound. I heard it. That's the sound."

"It's all right," Colm says. He rocks the door again. "It won't budge. I can't get it open. It's secure." He sets the stick into the channel of the sliding door.

"You can't, but what if he can?"

"Who?" Colm says.

"The man. It was him. I know it. He called her Gladys, not Gaddie. He was pretending." Beverly's voice is quiet. "He's trying to get in. What if he did get in? He left the lock open when he took the stick out. And now he's in and he locks the door behind him. He's in here, now, waiting. I know it." She sits down on the stair and twists the shoe in her hands. "Colm?" she says, looking at her husband.

An hour later, they are in bed again. At Colm's suggestion and to Beverly's relief, they have searched the condo from top to bottom, they have looked in every closet and cupboard, under every bed, behind every curtain. They have peered into crawlspaces, climbed in the attic, searched the garage. They have shone flashlights into every dark corner. They are alone. Colm lies on his back with his hands interlocked behind his head, staring at the skylight. The phone is beside his pillow. Beverly is pressed against him. They listen to the ticks and creaks, a gust of wind in the rafters, a squall of rain beating against the windows. Appliances click and hum, turning off and on in their duty cycles. Beverly rubs her tummy. She asks, "When will the baby move?"

Al's Book of the Dead

I. Writer

Al sold stereos. Lots of stereos. He was Regional Senior Sales Manager, Western Canada. Al was married, had a son, a daughter, a Labrador retriever, a Mercury Sable station wagon. Al sniffed cocaine, drank whisky, watched strippers in taverns. But that's not important.

Al was alive. That was the important thing. Because Al was writing a book. What separated Al from the people he wrote about was this: They were dead. He was alive.

Al's book was a kind of a list. It contained the names of all the people he ever knew who had died. The first entry went:

Diane Adams
I first heard Diane used a razorblade to scrape the

empty baggie from an ounce of coke and shot that, and the plastic from the bag got into her brain, then Stan W. told me no, she OD'ed on bad speed or MDA.

I liked Diane ever since I came on to her when we were about fifteen and she just laughed and laid a hit of acid on me. She went to New York to be an actress or a model or something for a while. She came back though.

II. Style

Al didn't know much about writing books. He didn't read, except for trade magazines and business reports, the occasional in-flight magazine, *Golf Digest*. He didn't know about plotting or character development or theme or conflict resolution or foreshadowing. He didn't know that even non-fiction books about dead people used narrative structures.

Al didn't know the kind of book he started to write had a tradition. He had never heard of William S. Burroughs or James Carroll or *Howl!* or Charles Bukowski or Crad Kilodney. He didn't know that someone born white and middle class in Jasper Place wasn't supposed to write a book about dope addicts and criminals and alcoholics and just plain ordinary people who happen to die.

So he wrote:

Kelly Shopstuk
Shopsy shot himself twice in the face. He was using a

cheap 22 and the first one didn't even go through his cheekbone so he went through his eye socket and blew his brains out.

He was up in Peace River living in a motel room with two of his cousins. He was up there trying to stay out of trouble but I heard from Val he was drinking bad after he got laid off.

P.S. Shopsy's brother I forget his name I didn't really know him died in that accident on Groat Road where that car fell off the overpass.

III. Manuscript

Since he was on the road at least ten days a month, Al found plenty of time to work on his book. He wrote in longhand, using a PILOT pen with either green or blue ink. He never wrote at home.

His handwriting was poor, but not illegible. He scrunched the pen between his index and middle fingers and overlapped it tightly with his thumb. The lowercase letters were cramped together on uneven lines. His capital letters were always printed, neat and square. Solid blotches of ink marked the spots where he crossed out a word or phrase. He sometimes tore through the paper.

He wrote the book on stationery from the hotels and motels of his sales trips. He collected the pages of his book in a large three-ring binder with a pale yellow plastic cover. The logo of an out-of-business stereo manufacturer decorated the spine. He kept it among similar binders of parts catalogues and product brochures on a bookshelf in his Vancouver office.

When he returned from a sales trip, he inserted any new writing into the proper place in the book. With a single exception, he wrote one obituary per page and filed them alphabetically by last name.

The exception read:

The Agostini Family
This is the only family I knew where everyone died.

Marc Agostini: Marco was found one morning in his car. They never knew whether it was on purpose or whether he just came home drunk and passed out with the motor running.

Marco was my age and we went to school and stuff starting about grade three. His house was a hangout when we were teenagers because Mrs. Agostini was never home and we could do anything in the basement. Also, Marco's oldest brother Rick had a Marantz stereo and a bunch of records. Slade, Uriah Heep, Deep Purple, Status Quo. We were really into that English shit. I always knew Marco had a tough time with his family but I never figured him for suicide. He bought a real expensive lamp made out of stained glass with his first paycheque after high school.

Mrs. Agostini: Mrs. Agostini burned herself up. It was Christmastime and I was visiting the folks. The couch she set on fire with her cigarette was left out in the front yard for a couple of days.

I never knew Mr. Agostini. He never came around. When Mrs. A died she was living alone in the house. Somebody tore it down and built a house like a big cottage on the lot.

Ricardo Agostini: I heard from Sheila R. that Rick died in a mining accident in Ontario. Rick was older by four or five years. We all figured Rick would turn out to be some big success.

Roberto Agostini ("Pee Wee"): Bobby died last year. He had arthritis or diabetes or something.

Bobby was a grade ahead, but was always really scrawny. He was a pretty good soccer player though. We used to get him to go tapping at the liquor store he was so pathetic looking. One time there was a bunch of us tripping on acid and Bobby couldn't remember how to tie his shoelaces and he freaked out and ran home in the snow without shoes. We went to call on him, ten or twelve of us wired out of our minds, and Mrs. A came to the door and told us Bobby didn't feel good and to go away. That kind of worried us so later Stan W. and Stevie Q. snuck back and talked him down through his bedroom window. He hated it when we called him Pee Wee, which was his nickname.

IV. Theme

This is how Al's book got started. He was in a Victoria nightclub called The Anvil, drinking with some clients. Low ceiling, loud music. Twenty-five years ago, he lived for nights in bars like this, pounding back double paralyzers, scarfing drugs by the handful, chasing after high school girls with fake ID.

The band in the club was doing a tribute set to Deep Purple, and halfway through the prolonged solo in "Highway Star," Al recognized the guitarist. It was Larry Murphy. Murph and Al had gone to Sunday school together, played on the same soccer team, had even shared a paper route for a while. Murph had been playing in bands since about grade eight. Al hadn't seen him in years.

During a break, Al bought Murph a drink. Sitting at a tiny table they made a peculiar pair. Murph was tall, skinny, all hair and pale skin and tattoos and bony shoulders sticking out of his black sleeveless shirt. Al was short, stocky, intense, with a golf-course tan; he was still in his suit and white shirt, his tie loosened. They talked for twenty minutes, telling tales about the old neighbourhood, catching each other up on their lives.

"Hey, you ever bump into Diane?" Murph asked at one point.

"Died," Al said.

"Wow. She's good people. She get sick or something?"

"OD."

"Bummer. That's just fucked. She was a cool chick." Murph lit a smoke and had a swallow of beer. Al noticed he still held his bottle in that weird way of his, gripping the long neck around his fingers like it was a cigar and tipping it up with his knuckles. "You hear about Shopsy?" Murph asked.

"No."

Murph made his finger into a gun and pointed it at his head.

"Fuck. When was this."

"I dunno. Last year. The year before. After Eddie. You knew about Eddie, right?"

"I was at his funeral."

"Hey, I was there. I don't remember connecting with you there, man."

"I didn't stay long," Al said.

That night, before he slept, Al wrote a list of names on the Strand Hotel stationery. It was his outline.

Many months later, in Winnipeg, Al had lunch with a client who specialized in heavy-duty sound equipment for concerts. He was a mutual friend of Murph and Al.

Larry Murphy

Murph caught double pneumonia. Phil T. from Winnipeg thinks it was AIDS. I only saw Larry once in the last ten or twelve years, just a little while ago. I remember he didn't look so good. Skinnier than ever. He was probably sick then, knew he was a goner. Maybe that's why he kept talking about all those dead people. The original rock'n'roll headbanger. I guess I owe this whole damn thing to him.

V. Reader

Al kept his book a secret for a long time. He had no reason for doing so, other than a vague sense of embarrassment at the thought of being a writer. And then too, he had no good reason to show it to anyone.

Sandra, he was sure, would not like it. She would think it morbid. She would worry, tell him that the past was not important when he had so much future to look forward to. She would sulk. She would argue. She would convince him to drop it. She would probably be right.

His family would find it disturbing. His wild youth, his drugs and drinking, his unsavoury friends. His mother and father were retired, they lived a quiet life. They wouldn't want to remember. His sister was a holy-roller now, she'd want to save him.

None of his current friends or business acquaintances would get it. The sharks at head office would see it as a sign of weakness.

Al finally showed it to his friend Stan Walker. Stan was a filmmaker, teaching at an art school in Toronto. He and Al still managed to hook up a few times every year. In the middle of the night during one of Stan's trips to Vancouver, Al took Stan to his office. On the drive there, he couldn't talk about his book. Al sat in the shadows as Stan read the book by the light of a desk lamp. At first, Al was nervous. He had never watched anyone read his work. As the minutes passed, his nervousness faded. He dozed off.

It was getting light when Stan finished reading all of the eighty-three pages. He embraced Al in a big bear hug and wouldn't let go. His voice a hoarse whisper, Stan said, "Most of us don't know shit about."

It was a line from the book:

Eddie van Dyk

Eddie went on a bender and never came back. Alcohol poisoning complicated by downers. He was dry for almost a year before that.

Everybody loved Eddie. I saw him the Thursday before he died when I was in Edmonton on a trip. Just dropped by his mom's place as I was driving by, and there was Eddie on the couch, watching the soaps and playing with his dog. I could write a whole book about Eddie. Once we had the same dream on the same night, about shooting stars and rocket ships in a 7-Eleven parking lot. One afternoon, I got Eddie out of bed to deal me a chunk of hash, and he said, "Some day I'm gonna die of a hangover." He was on and off the wagon a lot. He wasn't real good in school, but he was deep and took a lot of stuff seriously. He fought with demons most of us don't know shit about.

VI. Character

Unlike many of the people in his book, Al had never been busted by the cops. He had never been rushed to hospital with an overdose. He had never been suicidal. He had spent the better part of ten years in a lifestyle that killed and injured the weak and the strong alike, but Al survived. He liked to think it was because he was neither weak nor strong, just average.

His first impulse had been to document the most sensational deaths: all those suicides, overdoses and car wrecks. Even a guy he knew who was murdered. But as the book grew, he added entries that were ordinary by comparison. The cancers, heart attacks and strokes were no less deadly, just as random. That line between the here-and-now and the there-and-then was arbitrary.

The earliest death experience he could remember was this:

Sally Boychuk
Sally died the summer between grade seven and eight. She had a virus in her heart or something like that.

Sally was the most popular girl in our class. I had a crush on her most of grade seven. I even got to kiss her once in the shacks behind the hockey rink. She played the violin and went away to summer school all the time, except that last one. If it happened today they'd give her a heart transplant.

VII. Climax

A year and one hundred and thirty-one obituaries later, Al ran out of dead people.

After two months without an addition, Al was happy and sad. Happy that everyone else was still alive. But he had come to look forward to the book during his sales trips. He even toyed with the idea of making up the deaths of imagined characters.

He began to carry the whole book with him on the road. He would sit in hotel rooms, flipping through the pages. Occasionally, he would edit an entry, re-word a description, perhaps add a postscript. He started using a purple pen for the corrections, so he could keep track of the changes. He tabulated the various causes of deaths. He sorted the entries by name, by gender, by age. He compared the numbers.

One night at home, after four days on the prairies, he lay in bed with his hands clasped behind his head. "I never knew anyone who drowned," he announced. Sandra extinguished the light and crawled in beside him. "That's good," she said.

Two weeks later, Al started a new entry:

Stan Walker
Fell off a boat into Lake Ontario.

VIII. End

Al hunched over a table in The Anvil. For last call he ordered a beer, a Bushmills, a coffee, a Coke, and a water. He made notes on a napkin. He had an idea to write something, a movie or a novel maybe, featuring his dead people. It might help justify the existence of his book of the dead.

Since Stan's drowning, the liver failure of his father, and then the sudden brain cancer of his health-nut boss, Al had begun to chafe under the burden of maintaining the book. It scared him. As he grew older, the book would grow thicker. He felt like he was in a room where the walls moved closer when he wasn't looking, and his chest tightened whenever his mind thought of someone still alive who might one day be dead. As if just thinking about it could make it happen. Sandra. His kids. He needed that whisky. If he lived long enough, his would be the only name missing.

When the waitress brought his round of drinks, he gulped the

Bushmills then drained the water. As she cleared the table, she reached to pick up the napkins he was using for notepaper. Al gripped her wrist hard.

She twisted out of his grasp and gave him a look. "What's with you anyways, mister?"

"I'm writing," he said.

Misdirection

Ice tumbles out of the pitcher and into her glass as the waitress tops up her water. "Are you ready to order, or do you want to wait a few more minutes?" Viola checks her watch: almost an hour. She wonders if her daughter is at another restaurant. It's not that hard to do, really, she thinks. Like the time Vi got on the wrong bus for the cross-country ski outing. It could have happened to anybody. She saw the bus parked in the shopping centre across from the Jewish Community Centre. A gentleman stood next to it holding a pair of skis. She pulled up and rolled her window down a crack—it was bitterly cold—and asked him, "Is this the bus for the Kananaskis trip?" And the man said, "You bet." She parked her car, loaded her skis, and got on.

She wants water with no ice, but the waitress keeps crowding the glass with cubes. The lunch rush is slowing. Men in suits scribble signatures on credit card slips. A trio of bank tellers gathers purses and jackets from the backs of their chairs. The garrulous line-up of those waiting at the door has disappeared.

Her daughter Joy is never late, certainly not an hour. "Didn't you notice that there wasn't anyone on the bus you knew?" Joy had asked about the ski trip.

"Well, when I got on there were only two or three others. I didn't pay much attention, I guess." Vi had put on her headphones, loaded the tape of her talking book—they were doing a Maeve Binchy for her club that month—and took out her knitting. It was only when the bus stopped an hour and a quarter later—not at the William Watson Lodge but at the Delta Hotel—that she really noticed the absence of "my Jewish ladies," as she calls them. Most of the day-trippers were men. She discovered they were from the Shell Oil Retirement Club. "They treated me marvellously. They insisted I join them for the lunch they put on at the hotel after." She saved the sandwiches she had packed in waxed paper for supper that night.

She asks the waitress: "Can you please tell me what the specials are again?" It's a fishy something, Vi can't remember, she never cooks fish, it smells up the home so. Maybe tuna or salmon from a can occasionally, fish sticks when the children were still home. But the waitress has turned her head and banters goodbyes with a group of regulars. Vi looks at her water glass. Even her membership in the Jewish Centre was an accident. Her neighbour had told her about the daily drop-in aquasize classes at the Southland Leisure Centre, where seniors qualified for a fifty percent discount on a ten-visit pass. "Where was that?" she had asked; "Oh just down the road, you know the one."

The next time she was heading down 90th Avenue she stopped in. The customer service rep informed her, no, they didn't have a drop-in aquasize, they had a program for members only, no extra fee but pre-registration required, three times a week, not every day. Seniors did qualify for a thirty percent membership discount, but there were no ten-ticket passes. "I was told you do. I'm sure you've made a mistake," Vi said. By the time she left, the manager had agreed to sell her a full membership at a half-price discount. Two weeks later she realized the Southland Leisure Centre was the facility on Southland Drive, the other way from the house.

"You do this all the time," Joy said.

"Nonsense," Vi said. "Besides, how else would I have got to know my Jewish ladies?"

The waitress turns back to Vi, settling onto one hip, holding the water jug loosely at her side. "Did you want to order?" she says.

"The special," Vi repeats. "Could you tell me again what it was, please?" She half-listens to the list of radicchio salad in a vodka-berry dressing, Chilean sea bass with fennel and some sort of herb reduction, pilaf. Out of habit she lifts the flap on her handbag on the table to make sure her keys are there. One time she couldn't find them after a shopping trip to the Hudson's Bay store in Chinook Centre (she still calls it that, never The Bay, just as she calls the store at the other end of the mall Simpson's Sears). That was the trip where she bought the loveseat for the family room, the one she returned on the 89th day of the 90-day trial period. She was certain she had locked the keys in the trunk, phoned the Alberta Motor Association for the locksmith. She led him to a red Accord in the lot, watched while he slipped a thin piece of metal into the window frame and jimmied the latch. It was only when he popped the lock that she said, "But this isn't my car. Look, there's a baby seat in the back."

"You don't pay attention," Joy said.

"Pardon me?"

"You smile and nod, but you're somewhere else."

"That's a fine thing to say about your mother."

"I'm just not sure," Vi says to the waitress. She pulls her little phone book from her bag. She's not wearing her trifocals, so she raises her glasses off the bridge of her nose and peers under the rims. She checks under the J's for Joy, even though she knows she has never bothered to write down her daughter's cellular phone number.

She looks up and asks, "Do you have another location in the city somewhere?"

"Another location?" the waitress repeats. She doesn't look at Vi, her eyes are scanning the room, checking the hot line for any orders up.

"I thought perhaps this might be part of a chain," Vi offers. "Perhaps my daughter has gone to a different one." Years ago, before George left her for that other woman—they're both dead now, *bon débarras* as Grandma Mich used to say—she and George were to go to a Christmas party. A very classy affair, George in his dinner jacket, Vi in the dress that she had purchased for her sister's second wedding. From Chez LeMarchand, hundreds of dollars, a Parisian designer gown, two fittings. At the last moment, George phoned to say he was tied up in a conference with a client. "Meet me there," he said, "You'll know lots of people." She'd sent his evening clothes to the office by taxi. She didn't write down the address, she thought she knew the house, an old sandstone mansion in Mount Royal. Who knew there would be so many? They all looked the same in the dark as she drove up and down the streets. A limousine pulled into a long drive and a liveried footman stepped forward to open its rear door.

She parked—there was no street parking for nearly a full block. Wishing she had worn winter boots and carried her dress shoes in a bag, she picked her way up the drive, over the ice and ruts, thankful for the sand spread on the slope. As she neared the door, the footman came to meet her, umbrella held high to ward off nonexistent snow. "Good evening, ma'am," he said. "Welcome." He ushered her into a foyer that was open to the second floor, as big as the lobby of a grand old hotel. He helped her out of her coat and hung it in a cloakroom off to the side. She was greatly fond of that coat, a simple long cut made from good grey wool, but she saw it looked drab next to the furs on the rolling racks. A woman in a dress identical to hers, but accessorized with pearls and diamonds and platinum jewellery, broke off from a group and came to meet her. "I'm so glad you could come," the woman said. Their eyes swept each other, searching for recognition.

"Your dress," Vi said, and she laughed, a nervous giggle that never failed to mortify her. It rang so hollow. "Oops."

The other woman beamed a smile and took Vi's arm. "We have exquisite taste, you and I. Just wait until I talk to Georges."

"Pardon me?" Vi said. "Is he here?"

The woman lifted her eyebrow, what was left of it. "I'm sorry? Is who here?"

"George. Did you say George?"

The woman's smile slipped ever so slightly, then she went on: "Georges. Georges LeMarchand? Is *he* here? Heavens no. But you must have got your dress from his shop, n'est-ce pas?"

Vi giggled again, covering her mouth with her hand. She was aware that her only jewellery was a simple gold wedding band. She wondered if she should have worn gloves. "I thought you said George. My husband's name is George. Is he here yet? He was stuck at the office." The woman was looking over Vi's shoulder now. "Oh, I'm sure if he's not here, he will be soon." She disengaged from Vi to greet two couples coming through the door. "Clarisse, Joan. Hello. Andrew, Zachary." As she moved away she gave Vi a squeeze on her arm—a gentle caress just above the elbow, for which Vi was thankful.

Vi drifted from room to room, group to group, standing at the fringes of conversation, admiring the paintings on the walls, the books on the shelves, the statues in corners. The house was the biggest she had ever been in that wasn't preserved as a museum. People actually lived here. Vi wasn't even sure what to call the half-dozen rooms, plus hallways and foyers, where the ten-dozen or more guests circulated. The big one was the living room, she supposed, though its scale suggested a ballroom. And a library. A dining room, with the table pushed to one side and piled high with smoked salmon canapés and dishes of caviar flanked by rounds of rye toast and rows of tiny ivory spoons. Two more rooms she couldn't put names to. Dens? Parlours? Everywhere Persian carpets over polished dark hardwood. Mahogany? Ceilings at least twelve feet high, old-fashioned baseboards nearly up to her knee, flocked wallpaper, immaculate antique furniture. She tried to remember whose house it was—one of the new partners at George's firm? A client? A half-hour later, after sampling the caviar (surprisingly salty but clearly habit-forming) and dashing off two flutes of champagne proffered by silent waiters in long-tailed jackets, she found herself hovering near the front door, hoping for George. It was after nine o'clock.

Then the hostess was at her side again, still smiling warmly. "So. Still waiting for the mysterious George?" As she spoke, she spun a bracelet on her wrist.

"Oh. He's not mysterious," Vi said. "Just late. I was hoping to find a phone to see if he's still at the office. I'm afraid I don't recognize anyone here."

The woman guided Vi to a small room, hardly bigger than a closet, just off the entrance. A Princess telephone stood on a compact polished desk, along with a pad of linen notepaper and a pen in a marble holder. Vi pulled her little phone book from her clutch and looked under G. Though she called him at least once a day, she was no good at remembering numbers. She dialled his phone and, as expected, got the answering service. She tried the switchboard—again nothing. She called the security desk in the lobby of George's building and was relieved when Neil answered. He was one of the regular security officers, not some pimply-faced recruit filling a shift. "Neil," Vi said, "It's Mrs. Spenser. I was wondering if you knew whether George—Mr. Spenser—was still in the building." But no, he'd signed out an hour ago or more, dressed for dinner. She waited while Neil confirmed his exit in the log. "Thank you, Neil. Merry Christmas." She put the phone down. The hostess lingered nearby, rearranging a floral display beneath a mirror the size of the picture window in Vi's house. "No luck, dear?" she said to Vi.

"No," Vi said. "He left ages ago."

"Did I hear you say his name was 'Spenser?'" The hostess

looked at Vi in the mirror. "I'm afraid I just didn't recognize it at all." Vi felt the blood rush to her face, quelled the laugh that rose in her throat like an unwanted thistle in the garden. "Oh my. I think I've made a terrible mistake. I'm sorry to have put you out," Vi said. She had a sudden impulse to strike the other woman. She'd never told Joy that story. Never would either.

The waitress is saying, "No. We're not a chain. We're one of a kind."

Vi pushes her glass away. "I wonder if you can bring me fresh water, without ice this time," she says. The waitress grabs it quickly, spilling a few drops on the tablecloth. Viola wants to order the fish. Not with the sauce or reduction or whatever nonsense they call it. Just fish, and rice. And a small green salad, lettuce and things, without any dressing, certainly nothing with vodka. That sounds like a very nice meal. Joy will be sorry if she misses it.

But Viola doesn't order. She dabs the corner of her napkin where the water is beading on the linen. She looks up, catching the waitress's eye. "What do *you* think I should do?" Vi asks.

Ledge

Twelve storeys down, traffic has stopped. An ever-growing crowd of a few dozen spills into the street. I can see their faces as they turn their heads to look up. There's Bob Logan from Accounts Receivable — he's easy to spot with his green checked sports coat and his chrome-dome head. That's Manny from the mailroom beside him, his long greying ponytail bobbing with excitement. No doubt they're both coming back from lunch — picking their Sports Select numbers, a poker game maybe. They might've even dashed to the casino and back. They're probably making book right now, taking bets from the crowd. I can imagine Bob yelling, "Jump!" or "Don't Jump!" depending on which side of the action he's holding.

My window unit, like all the units in this office tower, is sealed, so I am unable to hear his or the others' voices. Nor can I lean out to see how the crowd is developing directly below on the sidewalk in front of this building. I do have a good view across the street, to the building with the crumbling sandstone façade. Facing me, a man is standing on a ledge at the same level as my office, three or four metres below the top of his building. He's wearing a dark-blue double-breasted pinstriped suit. The well-tailored jacket is still buttoned. He's got a ridiculous polka-dotted bowtie coming apart at his high collar. One trouser leg breaks perfectly over his shoe. Shoes as absurd as his tie: pointed black boots with elastic inserts on the side. They do have a nice shine. The other neat cuff has ridden up and lodged in the high top at his ankle. With those shoes, I am amazed he has managed to climb onto the ledge.

I am certain that Bob and Manny have a bet going—if not with the crowd, at least with each other. They have edged their way around to the far side, where they are talking to a cop. Maybe the cop wants in on some of the action, figures he's got an edge with inside information. None of the three—Bob, Manny, the cop—pay attention to the man. I look across again. He seems handsome enough, he's probably very attractive in spite of the tie and shoes. Maybe I think so because he's so vulnerable. His hair is blowing a bit in the breeze, across his fore-head, catching highlights from the summer sun. He could be in a shampoo ad. He's hanging on now above his head, both hands clutching the jaw of a gargoyle that adorns the parapet.

I have difficulty making out his expression as he looks down between his upraised arms. He is standing duck-footed, trying to maintain as much purchase as he can on the narrow ledge. He recoils as if startled, letting a foot slip, and I flinch too. A woman has appeared on the roof above him. I think she's called out to him. I see her lips moving. As he regains his footing and twists to look up at her, I finally see his face well. Sad-eyed with a furrowed brow, he has a lively mouth and chin. I would guess his age at mid-thirties.

The woman on the roof is talking. Even though she's in civilian clothes—a smart black blazer over a silky-looking green blouse with a big collar—I assume she's a cop. At least she's in the company of police who stand back out of the man's line of sight. I can just see the tops of their bodies above the edge of the roofline. Dressed in tight-fitting fatigues, they hold their leather-gloved hands cupped to earpieces. Coiled wires disappear into tight shirt collars. They talk into their sleeves and beckon to others I cannot see. The man on the ledge shakes his head.

When he puts his head down, I can see he's thinning on top. Not exactly male-pattern baldness, he hasn't resorted to combing long hanks over the top. But there's the shine of scalp. Then he looks up to see the woman on the roof. He crooks his right arm—still raised to the gargoyle's mouth—to make a port through which he peers at her as best he can. He exposes the whiteness of his throat as he tilts his head and raises his eyes skyward.

Two more observers have appeared at a window below him and a little to his left. One is a stout middle-aged woman in a brown outfit with epaulets. The other is a cop in regular uniform. The building on which the man is perched is turn-of-the-century vintage, so they can open the window and lean out. By the expression on the woman's face, I assume that she is the man's boss, or lover, or both. Or she wants to be his lover. I look over to try to make out whether or not he's got a wedding band on his left ring finger. She is calling to him, making beseeching gestures with hands and face. As the woman in brown leans forward, the cop looks at her cleavage.

The police helicopter beats the air overhead. Down in the street, the crowd numbers in the hundreds now. I can hear the low rumble of their white noise, muffled but steady through the triple glazing. The fire department is trying to set up an airbag, but a portico and a parked chocolate-brown delivery truck obstruct the impact zone. A fight has broken out on the edge of the crowd. I watch as the jostle of combatants and police and spectators eddy and swirl in the wash of the mob. I've lost track of Bob and Manny.

The man has managed to turn around so that he is hugging the building, still hanging on to the gargoyle above. His pants are smudged with dust, his shirt is untucked at the back and sticks out below his jacket. I think I can see a tear at the seam under his arm. Two cops on the roof are rigged like climbers with ropes and carabiners, ready to leap over the edge. The woman is leaning far over the parapet, held secure by fatigue-clad officers who have girded her with a safety belt. Her blouse is straining at the buttons, pulled taut over her slim bosom. She's wearing a matching green camisole. If the man released his left hand from the gargoyle, he might be able to grasp hers. The woman in brown below has her head buried in her arms on the windowsill. The cop beside her listens to his radio. The man looks back and forth between the proffered hand, the street below, and the woman in the window.

I wonder about taking a thick felt marker from my top drawer and writing a sign on a piece of my letterhead to hold to the window. What to say?

Don't Jump.

Choose Life.

Please.
It Can't Be That Bad.
Reconsider.
Jump.

My telephone rings. It's Bob Logan. "Wave to him," he says. His voice is digitally compressed. He's calling on his cellular. "What?" I ask. I scan the street below, and sure enough there's Bob among the throng, phone pressed to his ear. Both he and Manny are looking up towards me, but at the wrong window. "I'm over here," I say.

"Wave. Now. Just do it," he says and hangs up. I look across to the man, and for the first time he glances over his shoulder and sees me. Our eyes lock for an instant. He wriggles to turn himself half-around to see me better. The woman on the roof looks over, and the woman in brown lifts her head. One of the tactical team police officers across the way trains his binoculars on me.

I lift my hand as if I'll wave.

The Day the Buffalo Came

There was no shoulder on the road, just ditch, which is why I didn't pull over to take the picture. I really can't say why I wanted to take a picture of a dead horse in the first place. Startling image, I guess. Perhaps it was the sun and the heat— I'd been driving all afternoon with the sunroof open and it was hot, 34 or 35 degrees. That's maybe what killed the horse, heat prostration.

The corpse: charcoal-grey with Appaloosa spots on its rump and a black tail and mane, collapsed awkwardly, upside down, splayed feet pointing up to the crest of the knoll. Two more horses standing over the dead one: one looking like its twin, pawing the ground near its head, the other a skittish strawberry roan nickering near the tail. On top of the knoll, somewhat apart from the others, a black-and-white paint pony cantering back and forth against the backdrop of the Porcupine Hills and clear blue skies.

I down-shifted quickly from fifth gear to fourth. I glanced in the rearview—still plenty of separation between me and the farm truck I had passed a couple of minutes before. I have a bad habit, as dangerous as talking on a cell phone or eating a Big Mac while driving. Flipping through my catalogue of photos taken over the years, I can pick out dozens of pictures I've snapped from moving vehicles. Buildings, landscapes. People, cars, sunsets through the windshield. Keeping one hand on the wheel, I worked my camera free of the bag on the seat beside me and raised it quickly at arm's length, thumbing the autozoom and trying to frame a shot through the passenger window as I drove by. It's a move I've done a hundred times before.

I was listening to Jimi Hendrix on the stereo, god knows why, and it was loud. I think the horses could hear it too—the one on the hilltop reared up. Beautiful. Just as I snapped, I hit a pothole and some washboard in the road and fumbled the camera. I muttered a curse, grabbed it and lifted it again. I was more or less even with the horses now, maybe a bit ahead, so I leaned way over until the camera was almost out the other window.

Maybe I cranked the steering wheel to the left as I was pushing off it. I don't know. As I clicked the shutter and the Pentax's autowind whirred and Jimi's guitar wailed, I heard the horn and looked up.

I was on the wrong side of the road, veering for the nose of a motorhome with Michigan plates. It is peculiar, I know it is almost a cliché, but somehow I had the time to think, Wow, he's a long way from home. I yanked the wheel to the right and jammed the accelerator. I had slowed down so much that the engine lugged, and hesitated. The other driver was so close I thought I could touch him. He was sitting behind his windshield like it was the plate glass window at the Four Seasons in Manhattan. Fifty-five, maybe sixty years old, trim and tanned with neatly cropped white hair and a pale yellow golf shirt. I could see the alligator crest on it. I'll never forget the look on his face—not frightened, nor alarmed, nor excited, but determined. A set to his jaw, a slight furrow to his brow, steady blue eyes. He had the look of a man who had faced down those hard inevitable moments in life—laying off a shift of factory workers, locking a son or daughter out of the house in a fit of ToughLove, shaking the hand of the executive vice-president after signing his forced retirement. And now this inevitable moment: he was about to drive his 33-foot Pace Arrow head-on into a vintage Mercedes sport coupe. I have an idea how I looked: sun-burnt architect with flip-up sunglasses flipped down, covering saucer-eyed panic—seemingly cool as death loomed.

That's when it happened. Or didn't happen. Whatever. I have trouble with this part. Saying it. When I tell this story as anecdote, I lie. I tell a lot of lies. I never tell people that I was trying to take a photo at arm's length through the passenger window of a moving car on a busy, narrow rural road. A photo of a dead horse. I usually say I was scrounging for a tape—a Tracy Chapman tape, *Fast Car*. That gets a laugh, sometimes. And I tell them when I saw the motorhome, I managed to slam the car down a gear and speed out of the way as if I was Jacques Villeneuve. I tell them there was no way I was going to let that grim-faced bastard cream me. I tell the story, with lies, complete with pantomime and pulled faces. I tell them it was a miracle, but a miracle of lightning reflexes and finely tuned German engineering and sheer will. But the miracle was something else.

I'm trying to get it all down here, trying to write the truth of what happened. But I can't really say what that is—what is the empirical truth, what principles of applied physics and vector mathematics and geometry in action caused our two vehicles to miss each other? I don't know. I closed my eyes and covered my face with my hands at exactly the moment my car should have crumpled under the wheels of the motorhome. My life did not flash before me, blackness did not loom, no shining light beckoned. But I saw something: Against the sparkling salmon backdrop of my eyelids floated the apparition of an upside-down horse, a dead charcoal-grey Appaloosa with x's for eyes, a dead horse that opened its mouth and spoke to me a word in a language I had never heard but recognized, a word like the rending of flesh and bone, and before I understood it, the word turned to thunder and the horse flattened and the spots on its rump reared to life and charged towards me in a herd.

I jerked my eyes open. My car was back on the right side of the road, swerving for the ditch. I could smell the tire smoke and burning brake linings from the motorhome. I came to rest a hundred metres later, the nose of the Mercedes slanted down, the tail jutting up onto the highway. The farmer from the truck following behind pulled open my door, shook my shoulder. "Are you okay?" he asked.

I swiveled my head slowly. The world seemed washed with a

brilliant yellow light, as if a spotlight brighter than the sun had been turned on. A steady rushing noise whooshed in my ears. The new hay and grasses on the hills radiated, luminescent. A wavering heat mirage billowed from the broken asphalt. The brim of the farmer's cap almost touched my forehead. I stared at his full feminine lips, so out of place in the leathery face, and leaned forward wanting to kiss them. I smelled manure and sweat. The farmer's lips moved. "Are you okay? Turn that damned radio off." I realized it was the man speaking. I switched off the stereo.

My eyes adjusted to sunshine. I noticed my shades on the floor. The rushing in my ears was the chirping of crickets and the wind beating the prairie grasses.

Now comes another part of the story I lie about—or rather, never mention. A sudden urgent pain surged through my bowels. I struggled to free myself from my safety belt. "Easy does it," the farmer said, just like his bumper sticker, but I hopped out. I lurched around to the front of my car and dropped my trousers and squatted in the caked mud at the bottom of the ditch. I clutched the bumper and stared where a pair of hand-sized swallowtail butterflies were flattened into the grille. I discovered what it means to have the shit scared out of you. As my body relieved its tension, I chanted to the butter-flies, "Better you than me, better you than me."

As I relaxed, a wave of embarrassment washed over me. A crowd had gathered up the road, pointedly not looking my way. A car towing a trailer crept past; a boy stared out the window, then I saw him turn to his parents in the front seat, talking and pointing. The motorhome driver stood on the shoulder above and watched me. He held the same grim expression, but I thought I detected a glimmer of amusement in his eyes. I asked, "Could you get me the Kleenex from the glove box?"

I clambered up from the ditch. I smoothed the front of my pants, made sure my shirt was tucked in. Picked up my sunglasses and covered my eyes. My hands were trembling. I closed them into fists. I have a trick from my boarding school days that I still use. When I was a boy it helped me when I was really scared—of the school bullies, the headmaster, of Parents' Day visits. I call it the Fearless Raccoon. I close my mouth hard, and concentrate on how the muscles of my jaw feel. I imagine two walnuts in my cheeks, and that I'm a little fearless raccoon. Without being conscious of it, I realized I was doing it that day. My breathing steadied and I controlled the shakes. The man from the Michigan motorhome and the farmer hitched a towrope from the truck to the Mercedes and hauled the car back onto the highway. When they crimped the rear bumper, I dismissed it with a wave of my hand. I thanked the farmer, nodded to the motorhome man and ignored the gawking crowd. Traffic crawled past from both directions. I climbed in the car, changed the tape to something classical, then sped away.

II

I was on my way to the Head-Smashed-In Buffalo Jump Interpretive Centre. It was, I had been told by the Travel Alberta trip-planning consultant, the only United Nations-designated World Heritage Resource in Canada. The centre has won awards for its design, and so I took a professional interest.

I am an architect. So I keep telling myself. My small boutique practice specializes in doing a select few sprawling homes for the rich and the very rich. The rich trust me: I am one of them, and a dilettante, and the wealthy trust their own dilettantes. Some years I come close to breaking even on the business. Most of my clients are acquaintances of my father or grandfather or my famous uncle. Others know my mother's father and brothers, and still a few more know my father's second and third wives' families. Many mornings, as I perfect the knot in my silk tie, I try to hold my gaze in the mirror as I remind myself, "I am an architect."

I rarely design great buildings. It's true that the lions of architecture—Wright and Mies, Philip Johnson, Erickson here in Canada—did find willing patrons, true lovers of art and form, clients who indulged the artist, encouraged design with vision. The results may or may not be livable—bedrooms with columns in the centre of the room, glass houses in suburbs, bunker-like austerity. Livable, no, but living works of art, yes!

My own work is closer to a long progression of compromises through phases of conception, design and building. I respond to the whims of those who sign the cheques. If my client wants a Doric portico grafted onto a house that is otherwise postmodern, so be it. I state my objections, then I do what is asked, walnut-jawed. It used to annoy my ex-wife. Why don't you stand up to them, she would demand. You don't need their business. This is true: grandfather's trust fund provides well. Tell them what awful taste they have, she would say, as if bad taste is a crime. I'm not that good an architect, I would reply. I think she divorced me for my shrug.

Occasionally, an interesting commission comes my way. I was introduced to a retiring oil baron who wanted to build an estate in the foothills of the Rocky Mountains, using earth-sheltered design—essentially a building that is set into the earth, underground, or backed into a hill or cliff. I drove out from the coast to meet the client and inspect the site. He owned a remarkable property, perched near the eastern slopes, complete with creeks, blind canyons and yogic cattle content to bask on hillsides and chew their cuds. I admitted that I had no experience with earth-shelter designs, but the challenge intrigued me. He suggested I take a look at Head-Smashed-In. And so it was that I came to be driving a back highway on a sunny July day on the prairie. Taking photos of dead horses.

I have the prints of the two photographs here on my desk as I write. The first, taken as the car hit the pothole, is as one might expect. Askew. The sky occupies most of the frame, overexposed and burned almost white. In the top left corner is a dark blotch: the door frame of the car. Running from the centre of the bottom edge to about a third of the way up the right edge, the crest of the knoll defines the horizon. The head and forequarters of the paint pony burst from outside the frame. A very dynamic photo, with its unorthodox composition, its implied action, the rearing horse. The second photograph seems to contain nothing. When the technician at the lab developed the negatives, she assumed this one was a ruined exposure. I asked for a print: a mottled grey background peppered with eighteen seemingly random dark blotches.

III

I had imagined the Head-Smashed-In site as a sharp precipice with a yawning maw below it. I visualized a stampede of buffalo pitching to their deaths down a sheer rock face. Instead, if not for the interpretive centre, you could drive by without picking out the spot from the blocks of hills and deep-cut coulees that surround it. The edge of the escarpment is a soft hump among the foothills. The cliff drops away only eight or ten metres down to a green meadow that stretches in a long slope to a meandering creek.

At the base of the slope, cars and recreational vehicles crammed into the exposed parking lot. I found myself checking for Michigan plates. When I unclenched my jaw, my hands began to shake. Walnuts, I thought, raccoons. I concentrated on the reason I was there. I found my notebook and jotted a few notes:

> Glinting chrome, enamel paint, shimmering tarmac. Mob in T-shirts and neon caps moving to and fro across slope. Detracts from the understatement of the building. Compromise: public building in the middle of nowhere needs significant space for vehicle access. Nowhere to hide.

> Interpretive centre itself handsome piece of architecture from the exterior. Set into steep hills, angles, & exposed façades match the rocky outcroppings of surrounding landscape. Between each level native grasses planted, cover the structural elements.

At the bottom of the page where these notes appear, I've added a single comment, the only documentation of the incident on the road:

> Close call w/ a motorhome on drive in. Saw dead horse in field.

I parked in the overflow lot, even further away. As I locked up the car, a courtesy minibus pulled up. The driver was a plump, middle-aged woman. She called out in a flat, sing-song voice: "Give you a ride up the hill." Her round brown face broke into a wide smile. I read the name on her tag: Lenore.

"No. That's okay. I'll walk," I said. I realized I was mumbling through clenched teeth, so I added, "Thanks anyway, Lenore." My voice sounded loud.

Lenore shrugged. "It's a hot day." I shrugged back, then turned away from her and busied myself wiping down my camera. I heard her clank the door shut and drive away. I snapped a few photos of the exterior from beside the car. Some 250 metres to the right of the centre sat a squat prefabricated shed. I assumed (later confirmed by my tour) this was the actual buffalo jump; I learned that the shed protected the archaeological diggings at the site. I made the last entry that day in my book:

> Science and entertainment in conflict.

It *was* a hot day. By the time I climbed up the path to the entrance, my shirt clung to my back and stomach. I could feel the sting of perspiration at my collar and under the strap of my bag slung over my shoulder. My teeth were beginning to ache, especially the right side where I have had extensive restoration work. Crowns and root canals on almost every tooth. When I closed my eyes, the ghosted image of the spotted horse swirled in my view, and the echo of its word filled my head.

I was here to work, I reminded myself, so tried to focus on the architecture. I discovered that my bag was empty save for a half-full bottle of water. I had left my notebook and wiped-down camera at the car. I tried to make them out among the flashes of sun-baked chrome, concerned I had left them on the hood or the trunk deck. I dropped a dollar coin into a telescope on the wide stone patio at the entrance and checked it out. There was my car, sure enough. No sign of the camera or book. I figured that the items were either gone or inside the car, so there was no reason to rush back. Later, I found them in the back seat, where I had no recollection of putting them.

I bought my entry ticket at a glass booth that reminded me of a movie theatre. The baking heat of the sun bore down on the south-facing entrance without respite. I noted a huge overhead door like a warehouse loading dock facing one side of the patio—it seemed a strange utilitarian element, another compromise for a building with no back door. A few planters cast from a rough aggregate were scattered, filled with wilting annuals.

Inside, the air-conditioned cool was both welcome and uncomfortable. One of the guides handed me a map of the building and instructed me how to proceed. I bought a souvenir pen from the gift store, and wrote a note in the margins of the map: "Bldg intended for public access needs map and guide?" I checked the map, then asked the guide for directions to the restrooms, where I washed my hands and sprinkled water on my neck and face.

The centre is designed so that you begin the tour at the top and follow the trail of exhibits back down to the entrance. The levels cascade down through an atrium dappled by the interplay of light and shadows cast from the skylights. I followed the buffalo tracks painted on the floor and caught a ride up in the elevators.

Outside on the plateau above the jump site, the wind blew hard and hot from the mountains to the west, beating down the scrub grasses. The Old Man River snaked through its long wide valley to the south, its course marked by the shimmering willows and cottonwoods. An interpretive guide began to tell the small group on the plateau how his people had structured the hunt at Head Smashed-In, how they prepared for weeks for the day of the jump. His name was Thomas. His hair hung in long braids over each shoulder, and tassels decorated his pearl-buttoned shirt. He wore faded jeans and topside loafers. He spoke with patience to the tourists. Though I didn't hear the question that was whipped away by the wind, he gave an answer to a woman dressed in tennis whites: "I don't know, ma'am. None of our people have hunted buffalo for over a hundred years." There was no malice in his voice, no irony, no challenge. He stated it as simple fact.

As I worked my way down through the centre, I became distracted. I kept thinking I was seeing the man from the motorhome, wondering if he was following me, stalking me to exact revenge. For what? My tongue now was pressing hard against the roof of my mouth. The facility was too small, overcrowded with the throng of vacationing families. I scratched more notes in the margins of my map:

> Laser-activated displays, bilingual audiotapes English
> & Blackfoot languages. Space-age technology invokes
> lifeless replica. Stuffed buffalo poise at edge of 3rd level
> ready to leap down to cafeteria entrance on the 2nd.

I gazed up at these taxidermically-correct specimens. For centuries—perhaps a millennium—a culture had driven buffalo to jump to their death over a cliff. These carcasses had then been mined for food and tools. I stood in front of a diorama that attempted to explain Blackfoot mythology (only much later did I learn that the people at Head-Smashed-In called themselves Pikuni and Siksika, that those whom whites call the Blackfoot have their own names for themselves). These were peoples and cultures who knew nothing of silicon and iron and coal, who knew song and bone and dung.

In the air-conditioned box of the museum, I started to feel chilly, and I tried to rub some warmth back into my goose-fleshed forearms. I descended to the lowest level. Behind a Plexiglas wall, smudged with the fingerprints of the children of the day, the curators had meticulously prepared a facsimile of an archaeological dig—a facsimile of the very scene that existed in the squat hut a few paces away on the hill outside. Taut strings mapped a grid overlaying the replica. Excavations of varying depths pocked the arranged mounds of earth. Bones and arrowheads and shards of tools had been placed to give the appearance of randomness. Tools of the trade had been arrayed about the diorama: picks, spades, trowels, brushes, cement, plaster, calipers, rulers, notebooks, pencils. I stared at the pencils. Three of them: one angled across the black cover of a notebook. One dangling on a string tied to a clipboard. The third forming part of a triptych that also included a canteen and a pair of work gloves. We have pencils, I thought, but who uses them? Where are the people? I scribbled on the margins of the map what I think was the comment:

> Altar to scientific method, lacking only the celebrants
> to guide us.

But I'm not sure. The handwriting is so bad, it might say:

> Alter to science terrific or lucky only the cerebral to
> ground us.

Without the science of discovery could Head-Smashed-In Buffalo Jump exist? I overheard Thomas answer a question, that they find an average of three arrow points in a day's dig. I wanted to ask, who are "they"? If someone shoots an arrow and no one finds its point—whether the next day or centuries later—does that mean the arrow never existed? What about the man who shot it? The buffalo it killed?

At that moment in the concourse of the lobby, a group of drummers began to play and sing. The rhythm resonated in my breastbone. I turned away from the display and let the drumming pound into me. I didn't recognize the language of the high trebly voices; they sang a discord to my western ears, yet I thought I grasped a meaning to their singing. I let my jaw hang slack, unstuck my tongue from my palate. I felt my chin begin to quiver. Tears collected unbidden, and I closed my eyes. The vision of the Appaloosa materialized and the spots rushed towards me like a herd, and a word resounded inside me to the beat of the chant and the voice of the drum. I let loose a hoarse moan, almost a grunt. A young girl in a polka-dotted dress looked at me, and started to cry. She ran to a man and a woman who crouched down to comfort her. The girl pointed at me. The man stood up, and I thought I saw him taking a step towards me when I turned to leave.

I stumbled past the drummers, trying to find the way out. I glimpsed one of the performers, a youth. He was wearing a Detroit Tigers baseball cap, a black T-shirt with a Nike swoosh, jeans and Air Jordan sneakers. His face stretched with intensity as he sang and beat the drum. Grant. His nametag said Grant.

A lungful of hot dry air met me as I went outside. I blinked against the sunshine and wiped at my eyes. My hands were shaking. I licked the back of one and relished the fresh taste of salt. Lenore sat on a bench. There was no shade. She took a last drag from her cigarette, hoisted herself up, and ground the butt out. She nodded in my direction. It was just a nod, but it enfolded me like a hug. "Give you a ride down to your car?" she asked.

I understood the word, I know it still, when I answered, "Yes."

Sweetwater

The word "lake" stretching to two syllables, six children chanting as the station wagon passes the blank screen of the Sweetwater Lake Auto Cinerama: "I can see the laake! I can see the la-ake! I can see the la-ake!" Through the summer, day and night, the drive-in theatre shimmers like a beacon over the prairie, reflecting the blaze of daytime sun, catching projections of beach party bingos, Godzillas and war movie prisoners from dusk-till-dawn. At the turnoff to the lake, signs announce the Sweetwater Rodeo & Jamboree. The rodeo grounds decked with bunting, manure smells mingling with hot dust, pickup trucks and horse trailers and pitched tents scattered in the cactus flats. The clang of bells on bulls' necks, nickering horses, Marty Robbins whistling through the PA speakers.

Sweetwater Lake cannot be found on any map. There are no roads in: only paths of memory. A drive-in theatre still stands, where I watched Red Line 7000 *and* State Fair. *The things I cannot change. My brothers and sisters and I spread a blanket on the ground, sat under the stars, spellbound by images forty feet high. Crickets chirped the soundtrack. There was a rodeo every year.*

The lake itself still some miles distant, nestled out of sight in the clutch of drumlins. Yet they chant, "I can see the la-ake! I can see the la-ake! I can see the la-ake!" Six children, ages 6 to 18; three boys, three girls. One set of twins (the eldest siblings M-F fraternal), one daughter adopted. Mother and father: home-maker and physician, sun-dressed and sport-shirted. She, joining the children's chant, hands resting on plump belly. He, driving, hands on the wheel at ten and two, left arm sunburning through the open window. A brand new metallic grey 1964 Ford Fairlane station wagon, the colour of stainless steel, trimmed with chrome plate, pulling a rising plume of dust behind on the narrow, arrow-straight gravel road. In the rear-facing jumpseat in the very back, the youngest child, a boy, joins the rest, "I can see the la-ake," the will of his voice conjuring a body of water, when his eyes see only dust.

Am I that boy? When I write, "the will of his voice conjuring a body of water," the voice is the scratch of pen on paper, the water a flow of ink. As a boy, I passed a handful of summers in a two-room, rough-built cottage, perched by a lake. It was named something like Sweetwater Lake. An oasis on the prairie, spring-fed, with a natural beach of riffled dunes, ringed by bluffs of poplars with trunks as thick as I was. But this lake, Sweetwater Lake, is not that one, another name. That boy is not me. Did now-me exist in then-boy? Only in the me of memory, scattered in me or my. Mouthfuls of hot sand, chokecherry jelly, the screech of the water pump being primed in the springtime. I caught my hand in the tailgate of a Fairlane station wagon at that lake; my father stitched up the gash. I can feel the scar on my right thumb as it presses the pen. I sat in a jumpseat in a station wagon, watching dust billow behind. I called out for a lake, I pleaded to see water. I am 39 years old. God grant me.

On that last trip to Sweetwater Lake, stopping in Elgin, at the B-A gas station. Hamburgers and onion rings in the restaurant. Jimmy the pump jockey fills the tank and scrapes grasshoppers from the windshield. The eldest sister, Betty, flirts with him as usual, attracted by James Dean looks. His left arm missing, lost to a hay baler. Betty and her twin brother Dallas will leave for college in the east in the next week, and she will never see Jimmy and his stump again.

Near Wonderful, the father spies a golden eagle and stops the car. The family piles onto the shoulder of the highway, eight people shade their eyes from a sky more yellow than blue. The bird rides the updraughts ever higher, drifting into the sun.

Are there towns in Saskatchewan named Wonderful and Elgin where an eagle flew and a one-armed boy pumped gas? Did he wipe the windshield of a station wagon the last time we went to the lake? Did my sister flirt with him? I am 39 years old, but today is my first birthday. I remember this: as a boy, I went with my family to a cottage by the lake. Occasionally we stopped in a town with a name similar to Elgin and a young man with one arm pumped gas. My oldest brother and sister went away to college. I know we sold our cottage by the lake and moved to a city. There are brothers and sisters, but no twins. Only doubles. We once went to a lake, then stopped going. There were annual rodeos. I remember the cowboy.

The boy eating a hotdog wrapped in a slice of white bread. The cowboy knocks at the frame of the door with his boot. Backlit by the evening sun, a tall silhouette, as if two-dimensional, booted, hatted, the screen eclipsing details of texture and colour. The mother opens the door and he steps into life, rangy and ropy, all angles and creases. Into the kitchen: the smell of horse sweat and hay, whisky and liniment. With his left hand, he holds his right arm awkwardly, folded up beneath his chin.

The boy gapes. He stops chewing, breathing, takes it all in. Pointy boots caked with dung, jeans smudged and worn. The faded shirt burnt-orange and white, checked like a tablecloth, with pearly buttons. Face like leather, cut deep in the jowls, permanent squint shielding dust-pale eyes. The cowboy tilts his head back so that he can see under the bent brim of his woven hat, stretching the wattle of his neck tight over a knot of Adam's apple. He darts his eyes about the room, a nod to the mother, a wink at the boy. His smile rides up one side of his face to show gaps where teeth are missing. The boy looks away from his face and stares hard at the outsized belt buckle, where a bronze cowboy spurs a silver bronco. Lettering there: "Bareback Denver 1958."

With a sound like a bell, the cowboy half-hollers, "Is the doc around? Pete at the hotel said a doctor was here." The father: up in the loft napping, but awake now. He sticks his head over the edge. "I'm Dr. Leonard," he announces, fumbles for his glasses, then stretches the wire temples around his ears. The doctor puts on his black-bag face.

(Re)constructing the myth of father-physician. I was barely seven years old when my father traded the practice of medicine for the paper shuffle of hospital administration. Yet how I have clung to that myth! Did I ever believe? Do I still? I admit that I. The knock at the door, the honk of a horn in the street, the middle-of-the-night phone call, my father then grabbing the black bag and flying from the house. Broken-boned cowboys. The thousand babies born. Father-physician mythmaking. What can I comprehend of doctors' strikes and small-town politics? Of botched appendectomies? What wounds were inflicted untangling the corpses of friends from the mangle of farm implements? I know the scar of memory tracing the stitches in my thumb.

The cowboy: "I just busted up my arm." Dr. Leonard crawls down from the loft, plucks his bag from the high shelf in the pantry. The mother fusses over the cowboy: "Let me get you a chair. I've got some fresh lemonade, just made. I was just going to brew some coffee, would you like some?" The cowboy refuses all. He stands, swaying slightly, two steps inside the room, holding his arm.

Mother to the boy: "Now Marty, go on in the front room so you don't get in your dad's way."

"In your dad's way." When I was 24 years old, and my mother

was in the hospital recovering from a quadruple bypass, my father levelled his gaze at me. "Don't come between me and my wife." An overarching pronouncement: mythic, biblical, menacing. His words circumscribing a story in which I was not a character. Am powerless over. Mother as facilitator: micro-managing the dynamics of six children, mother and father. The keeper of secrets, the maker of myths. What do I remember, what do I make up? What was made up for me, the fictions of family rote-learned in the cradle? Where was my father when I was born? At home, asleep.

"Aw, M-m-mom," the boy pleads. "C-c-can I stay?" He has not taken his eyes from the cowboy. None of his brothers and sisters are home. The cowboy is all his.

"He can stay." The father not looking up as he searches in his bag. "He'll be all right."

The doctor washing his hands in a basin of water the mother has poured from the kettle on the stove. Methodical: fingers first, the webs between, the palms, the backs, the wrists. Then motioning the cowboy to stand near the table. The mother has whisked away the dishes and stripped off the tablecloth. A clean bath towel over the surface, stacks of clean washcloths. "So, what have we got here?" the doctor asks.

The mother carefully works the shirt off over the cowboy's injured arm, peeling it away from a xylophone of ribs playing under pale skin. A dark V at the neck, burnished forearms. The cowboy: "Not riding the rodeo, gave that up years ago." The story: handling a string of bucking horses for a stock contractor, moving them around the circuit. A Brahma bull breaks loose from the chute that afternoon and slams the gate back into his shoulder. "Slipped in a pile of horseshit—pardon my speech, ma'am," he says to the mother, winks again at the boy.

The doctor: "I'd need an x-ray to make a certain diagnosis, but you've probably fractured your clavicle—that's a broken collarbone—and you've separated your shoulder—sort of pulled it out of joint."

"I figured as much. Oh yeah. Busted bones before." Barking a little laugh. "Broke my back once, too."

"I'll bandage it and make a sling. You should try to refrain from using your arm or straining yourself for at least thirty days, sixty would be better."

The cowboy rubbing his chin with his good hand. The skritch-skritch of whiskers. "I'm heading for Oyen next weekend, then down towards Montana. I gotta keep working. Gonna be a piece of work to handle stock with one arm." He flashes his gapped smile, looking off into the distance of the far wall. Wheels turning behind the dusty eyes, working the angles. "Maybe get some of the boys to give a hand. Can't quit working."

The doctor bandages the shoulder. The wide adhesive tape as white as the flesh it covers, running over the ribs, a cloth placed under the arm, the shoulder pulled back a bit (the cowboy winces), the upper arm taped to the torso. The cowboy keeps talking: "With this get-up, you're making sure I don't move my arm—Good turnout this year at the grounds, yes ma'am—Hard to figure, but no, not so many injuries as you might think—The weather's good for the crowd in the grandstand, but you best watch your animals in this heat." The cowboy reaches his good arm across the table and tousles the boy's hair. "You're a quiet little one. What do they call you? I'm Stricklin, but everyone calls me Stick."

The boy stammering, "M-m-my name's m-m-Morden. Or m-m-Marty." He repeats, "m-m-Morden . . . m-m-Marty."

If you ask me, "Do you stutter?" I can state: "I have never stuttered." I do not tongue-grope the consonants that shape my history. My pen stitches a row of m's—I hold the key on the keyboard—

mmmmmmmmmmmmmmmmmmmmmmmmmmmmmmmmmmmmmmmmm
My initial, the m of me, hums from my lips. The me of memory sputters. The serenity to accept.

The boy's hand out to shake the cowboy's, a hesitation when right meets left. The cowboy grabs and pumps. "We call this the one-wing shake." Palm rough, like a splintered fencepost. The boy: "Your b-b-buckle's as old as m-m-me."

The cowboy answers: "Izzat so? I w-w-won it in a p-p-poker game." Another barking laugh. The boy's hand back in his own lap. He rubs it on his short pants, wiping away the touch of cowboy. The boy moves away from the table to stand by the propane refrigerator.

The doctor rigs a sling. Triangular bandage, wide under the elbow to cradle the bent arm high on the chest. "Try to keep this on, at least until Labour Day." Exchanging looks: they both know it will be off next week. "And have it looked at now and again until the pain abates—until it doesn't hurt so much." A scribble of prescription the cowboy says he doesn't want, but the paper tucked into a jeans pocket. "I'm quite serious. The collar-bone will be fine—sore for a while, but fine. But that shoulder may never heal if you're not careful. You'll pull it out trying to put your boots on."

The cowboy nods. The mother fusses the shirt, tucking the lame arm inside. The doctor washing his hands again. The boy slinks further into a corner. The cowboy: "How much do I owe?" The doctor: "It's not necessary. I'm on vacation." The mother: "Stay for supper, please." The doctor holds his wet hands up expectantly: "Marty, get me a towel." The boy fetches a towel from the table, moving between the awkward dance of mother, cowboy, shirt and father-physician.

Sudden silence and stillness. Three snaps on the bottom of the shirt the best that can be done. The father's hands dry, towel thrown in the sink. The mother poised between the cowboy and the table, as if there's something more to be done. The boy stands by his father.

Where do I stand? The scene plays itself out on the screen of my memory, the images (re)collected and transformed. Like a motion picture camera, my gaze tracks around the room, zooming in on detail, craning overhead. I do not exist. At Sweetwater Lake, I can place the boy beside the father, perhaps one step to the side and a half-step behind. But at that other, unnamed lake, where do I place the self? Where does the self place "I?"

The cowboy in motion: "Let me pour you a drink, at least." He plucks a couple of tumblers from a shelf, slides to the table. Glasses down, he hitches up one leg on a chair, draws a half-empty flask from his boot, spins the top deftly from the bottle, letting it fall to the floor. An economy of motion that belies one-handedness. Whisky drained from bottle to glasses, flask tossed flat-down on table.

The father: black-bag face closed tight. The shiny skin over his cheek rippling as he clenches his jaw, then relaxes, and clenches again. The father takes a step forward. The mother slips between the father and the table. The father seeing through. Sharp clack: the mother's teeth together as she draws her mouth closed. The boy glances from bottle to father to mother and back to the bottle on the table. A turn on her heel, the mother moves stiff-legged to the other room. Calling out: "Morden. Come with me." The boy remains.

Neither man smiles. Clink of glasses, whisky sliding into their mouths, down their gullets with a gulp. They do not speak. Burning gasps. They do not look at the boy. It is the first time the boy has seen his father take a drink.

The last time I saw my father take a drink: the day that he died. Physician-father. (Un)mythmaking. Alcohol. Where are the bottles of my childhood? In cupboards bare, in empty suitcases, in the trunk of the car. In the bole of a tree, under the eaves, buried in the ground. In a boot top, in the lining of a jacket, in a black bag. The first time I saw my father take a drink: he'd patched a broken cowboy at that other lake. Today is my first birthday, 365 days since step one: I admit that I am powerless over alcohol. I am 39 years old. I remember the cowboy.

The mother: "Marty. Marty, come on in here." Her voice soft, far away. The boy puts one foot in front of the other, then another and another and another. He is out of the kitchen. The front room: the mother is folded like an S on the couch, sitting in one corner, legs tucked under thighs, shoulders sloped. Bare knees almost covered by Butterick sundress. One listless hand plucks threads from the nap of the upholstery. Out the window, the pink and orange sunset casts the dark across the still waters of Sweetwater Lake. A boat speeds by, towing the twins for the last ski of the day. On the beach, a brother and a sister pat sand-cake ramparts.

The chirp of the spring on the screen door in the kitchen, as it expands and compresses, the rattle of wood and mesh as it closes. The sound of the station wagon starting up and driving away towards the hotel beer parlour. The boy reaches, fingertips touch his mother just at the hairline.

My daughter reaches to touch my brow. She points to each part of my face, and recites the naming game she has learned from her grandmother, that I learned from my grandmother. My forehead: "Fore-bumper," she says. An eye: "Eye-blinker." The other: "Hood-winker." "Nose-smeller." "Mouth-eater." My daughter touches my chin: "Chin-chucker, chin-chucker, chin-chucker." Her tiny fingers tickle at the lump in my throat. Today is my first birthday.

The Man in the CAT Hat

"Don't worry about it. That's just the way he thinks — " The man who spoke wore a CAT Power Equipment hat. He turned from one of the rust-stained urinals. The other man wore a neck brace and stood in front of a row of mirrors that formed a realistic frieze along the wall above the sinks. The man in the CAT hat quit talking when he saw the poet enter the restroom. The man with the neck brace also saw the poet. He looked away from that illusion and examined the illusion of a blemish on his reflected face. The poet staggered to the centre urinal and noisily unzipped his fly.

The man in the CAT hat went over and stood beside the man with the neck brace. He looked in the mirror at himself, at the man with the neck brace, at the back of the pissing poet.

Urine splashed steadily on stained porcelain. The two men at the sinks fidgeted. The room, usually filled with the violent melodies of argument, filtered jukebox, dope deals and running water, was silent. The man in the CAT hat and the man with the neck brace swallowed their words as they came up in their mouths. The man with the neck brace, thin and pale, drew a broken comb through thin pale hair. He watched the reflection of the poet turning towards him from the urinal

(who was me, drunk, ever-so-sensitive to reality: I had walked into the toilet and saw two guys, one doing up his fly and saying, "Don't worry about it, kid. That's just the way he thinks," and the other standing by the sinks toying with his neck brace. Making sure I didn't stare or seem to be paying attention, I swaggered to the urinal to the left and quietly unzipped my fly. I focussed on this living vignette, trying to fix an image of the situation from the inadequate sensory information I could glean from my surroundings. On the chrome elbow of the urinal pipe I could make out the funhouse image of two men facing each other. Through the wash of water and muffled bar noise, I heard the breathing of the two men as they mumbled: one hard and even, the other raspy and sick. I heard the soft whisper of a broken comb passing through Brylcreemed hair. My sensitive ears heard all, my sensitive eyes saw all. I turned from the urinal and looked straight into the reflected eyes of a man by the sinks)

and he said, "I dunno. Maybe I'm paranoid."

Knucklehead

Zelle @ 18 months

He will build a fence. The highest fence allowed by law. A thick, high, soundproof impenetrable fence. A fence without chinks or cracks between boards. He will allow no knotholes through which to peer, no handholds or footholds on which to hoist oneself. A fence sunk into the ground under which no small dog, no rodent, no child can burrow. A Berlin Wall, a Great Wall of China, a Hadrian's Wall, a Maginot Line. When he finishes the fence, he will plant a high hedge, a hedge that will grow skyward past the fence, past the height of the house itself. A thick, high hedge.

He has downloaded the development permit application and all the necessary supporting documents from the city website (the same website where he accessed the Animal Control Bylaw). He spends every tidbit of spare time planning and designing the fence. He uses his laptop and the CADD tools from his work. He knows how much concrete he will need for the foundation and the pillars, how many pallets of cinder blocks, how much sand, how many cubic feet of earth he will need to displace. He knows how much it will cost. He develops a budget and a construction schedule. He refines the design, consults his engineering references, revises and revises again. The fence will be a marvel. The fence will be a neighbourhood landmark. He will name it.

One morning, Colm lies in bed, staring at the ceiling growing lighter in the dawn's twilight, visualizing his fence. Beverly is still asleep beside him, curled around a pillow so that her spine presses against his ribs. He listens to the sounds of the house. Zelle in her room: she is awake, playing in her crib, singing to herself, talking in her own language to her teddy and monkey. Doxie's toenails click on the tile in the kitchen as she moves from her bed by the back door to the dog dish. He can hear her lap water. It is just a few days past the fall equinox, and without looking at a clock, Colm places the time at ten to seven.

He hears the Harley next door sputter to life. It's the wrong day, he thinks. Sunday is the day his neighbour starts his bike, not Saturday. And it's too early in the morning. Anything is possible these days. His dog poisoned, his car stereo stolen, twice. His garbage cans on fire. The phone stopped ringing mysteriously only because he opted for call screening. He has subscribed to a security service that has alarmed the doors and windows of his house and garage. The fence is next. He will break ground in the spring. He needs all winter to save the money.

The motorcycle next door has been slipped into gear, and he listens as the percussive slap-slap of the engine drives away, then hears it coming around closer again to the front of the house. His curiosity is piqued. In the last year and a half or so, he has never seen it ridden. His neighbour, Ted Cope, just starts it and lets it run. He never rides it anywhere. Colm gets out of bed and peeks between the slats of the blinds. It is not Ted but another man astride the idling bike in front of the house next door. Helmetless, approximately the same size, age, shape and colouring as Ted, but with short hair and a neatly trimmed goatee. Ted is standing on the lawn. He's wearing work boots and decent jeans, and a lined denim jacket. The bark-less terrier stands on the lawn, tethered to a leash which Ted has secured to his belt loop. As the man shuts off the engine and dismounts, Colm realizes he is wearing a leather vest with the patch of the most feared outlaw motorcycle gang in the world.

"Oh boy," Colm mutters.

Beverly shifts, and rubs her eyes. "What's going on?"

"You'll never believe it."

Beverly doesn't answer, she just rises and gets on with her day.

By eight o'clock, a half-dozen cars and pickup trucks have parked on the street. The Harley has been pulled up on the lawn. A dozen or fifteen men mill about in Ted's back yard next to Colm and Beverly's house, drinking coffee and beer. Boxes of Timbits are stacked on a table. Colm peeks out one of the windows and watches a man with a shaved head and a snake tattooed on the back of his neck toss bits of chocolate donut to the terrier and to Ted's other dog, the rottweiler.

"What is going on over there," Colm says.

"Why don't you just go ask, for christ's sake," Beverly says. She's wiping the porridge and pancake syrup from the table. Zelle is banging on her xylophone.

At nine o'clock, a delivery truck from Home Depot arrives. Someone moves the motorcycle again, and the men form a work line to unload the truck. They stack four-by-fours, two-by-fours, sheets of plywood, boards in piles. Beverly pulls her jacket on, grabs her purse. She has her keys and a grocery list in her hand. Zelle runs over to grab her leg. "Mommy, Mommy. Car. Me car." Beverly picks up Zelle and kisses her. "No, baby Zed. You stay with Dad. Mommy's going shopping."

Zelle starts to cry then pushes away. Colm comes over to take her. He kisses Beverly. "Don't forget the kiwi."

"Got it on the list."

"And the coffee beans."

"Right.

"Soy milk."

"Mmmm. See you in a couple of hours."

"Why don't you go for a coffee or something too? Spend the morning at Chapters? Zelle and I'll be fine, won't we kiddo?" Colm looks to the child in his arms. She's rubbing her eyes.

"I might," Beverly says. She kisses Colm and Zelle again and leaves.

Colm watches from the window, coaxing Zelle. "Say 'bye-bye, Mom.' Bye, Mom." Zelle isn't crying, but her bottom lip is curled. She buries her face in Colm's shoulder. Colm pulls a Kleenex from the pocket of his shirt where he always seems to have one, wipes her nose, then puts it back. A couple of the men look up from their work to check Beverly out. One of them says something and Beverly stops as she opens the car door. She's smiling and says something back. The men laugh and she does too. She gives a little wave of her hand to them, gets in her car and drives away.

At ten after nine, Colm glances out the kitchen window. They are pulling down the chain-link fence between his house and Ted's. Colm scoops Zelle up from where she's banging her toy train on the floor and heads out the back door, Doxie at his heels.

"What are you doing?" he demands. "What are you doing to this fence?"

A man with a pair of wirecutters straightens up. Colm realizes it's the Hell's Angel, he's just not wearing his patch. His T-shirt has a slogan on it: Any Questions, Dickhead? The man smiles. "Hey, you're just in time to help us out here. I'm Dave." He holds out his hand to shake.

"Help?" Colm shifts Zelle to his right side.

She's pointing to the tool in the man's hand, trying to lean over and grab it. "That? That, Daddy?"

"Help with what?"

"Building a fence," another man says from the deck.

"Tell him I don't need any help." Ted's voice, coming from inside the house through an open kitchen window.

"You can't," Colm says. Zelle is squirming, wanting to get down. Doxie sniffs cautiously at a gap in the fence. Ted's rottweiler rattles the chain at its neck, but stays where it is under a chair. Colm can't see the terrier, but hears its strange soundless bark inside. "You can't build a fence."

"We are," says the man with the snake on his neck. Ted comes to the back door of his house. "Ask him if he's going to call the City on us," he says to Dave.

The men laugh.

"You can't build a fence. I'm going to build a fence," Colm says.

Ted shakes his head. "Tell him he'll be gaining some real estate. Jim figures the property line's six inches my way."

Dave looks at Colm. He smiles again, a big grin that shows off a gold crown and good straight teeth: "You going to help us out here, or just get in the way?"

■   ■   ■

Zelle @ 3 weeks

Colm and Beverly close the deal on their bungalow over a year before Doxie is poisoned, when baby Zelle is less than a month old. Crestview is a blue-collar middle-class neighbourhood— there's not really a crest, just a slight elevation; and some houses with a second storey have a view of the mountains to the west. Beverly and Colm discover if they stand on their tiptoes at the edge of the deck and look south between the tree branches, they can make out what might be the edge of the town, or at least the green belt of Fish Creek Park. The demographics of Crestview are changing—the families who baby-boomed this suburb in the 1950s hear their own echo in the 1990s. Zelle is the first baby on their block in years.

After traipsing through dozens of houses, after returning to the bank (twice) to increase the value of their pre-approved mortgage, after endless arguments with Colm's mother Gaddie about all things house-related, after despairing that they will never find a home that isn't sitting on a pile of mud in the middle of a field a farmer harvested just last fall, that doesn't smell like an athletic bag full of hockey equipment, that isn't too small to rock a baby bye-bye, too expensive to afford mortgage, utilities,

134

furniture and groceries (pick the best three out of four), or too close to a fire hall (Beverly had grown up across the street from one, and hated the constant sirens)—after all this and more, they immediately fall for the bungalow. Their realtor is visibly relieved when they begin to talk about the conditions of the offer to purchase before they even see the basement.

Their house, and the one next door, stand out from the postwar sameness of the architecture in the rest of the neighbourhood. L-shaped, a little bigger than others nearby, the two houses have arched multi-paned windows and front verandahs flanked by clinker-brick columns. They look like they were built before the First World War, not after the second. Twin brothers from Scotland, Glaswegians and admirers of Charles Rennie Mackintosh, built their twin houses using plans purchased from the back pages of *Modern English Cottages*. The seller of their house—Nancy, the widow of one of the twins—takes pains to explain the houses are not identical, and neither were the builders. "For one thing, they're mirror images, the layouts. My Geordie was tall and handsome and fair. Jock was short. I've kept up the hardwood, and all the woodwork that the boys worked so hard on. Like an old-country place they used to say. Lydia modernized when Jocko died, in 1982. Wall-to-wall broadloom. Taking the wood out. My husband was a teetotaller, you know, never touched a drop. And our back door and staircase to downstairs are in completely different places. And of course the basements— Lydia lets Ted do whatever down there. My sons have all moved on. Teddy's still at home with Lydia, and her old mom too. Now that Geordie's gone, I'll go to the coast to be near my grandchildren. I've got two of them no bigger than little Zola here."

Nancy's home—soon to be Colm and Beverly's—is well kept. The cotoniaster hedges are trimmed as smartly as a sailor's haircut. On the spring day that Colm and Beverly tour with the agent, while Zelle bawls in the baby sling, the blossoms on the apple trees rain down sweet petals. Tulips in all colours bloom in flower beds by the front door. In a small, neat rectangle of rich earth in the back, the spinach and lettuce are already leafed out, and the feathery wisps of carrot tops have broken the soil. The near-identical house next door isn't exactly a dump, but needs new paint, and the shingles on the roof are starting to buckle, and there is a path worn across the front lawn where somebody takes a shortcut to their vehicle—it makes Colm and Beverly's choice look that much more appealing.

Colm and Beverly and the realtor and Zelle (quieted only by her mother's breast) sit in the realtor's Lincoln and draft the offer then and there. Later that night, after Zelle has been lullabyed into submission, they receive the phone call that their offer has been accepted.

◼   ◼   ◼

Zelle @ 14 months
[*The veterinarian describes how the dog lost its bark.*]
The terrier's name is unknown to me, and is recorded only as the name of its owner, Mr. Edward Cope, also known in our files as Teddy Cope. Mr. Cope submitted said terrier to us at the Noah's Ark Animal Clinic [*the same clinic to which Colm rushed Doxie after finding her under the deck*] with instructions to perform such surgical interventions as were necessary to render

the dog mute, such being one of the terms and conditions under which the authorities would release the dog to his custody. As the principal partner in this practice [*Dr. N. Lambert, the same vet who treated Doxie*], I attempted to dissuade Mr. Cope from such a course of action [*Dr. Lambert diagnosed Doxie as suffering from poisoning, likely from the accidental ingestion of a pesticide such as Warfarin or even strychnine*]. But after discussion with Mr. Cope, who forcefully and with invective inveigled upon me that he was within his rights as a pet owner, that he knew his own mind, and further that God gave dominion over the animals to man, I agreed to comply with his wishes. I performed the procedure to sever the vocal chords myself. Mr. Cope of course was not present with his dog during the operation. [*While Colm held Doxie, one of Dr. Lambert's assistants pumped the dog's stomach, then administered a dose of charcoal.*] For at least the past ten or even twenty years, Mr. Cope has conducted his business via telephone, and transports his pets to us in a kennel by animal taxi. Not infrequently, one of our staff will offer to pick up or drop his pets for him. In this particular instance, he arranged the transportation from the Animal Services Confinement Kennel. He never accompanies his animals; he hasn't since he was a teenager. I believe he rarely, if ever, leaves his house. Mr. Cope paid the bill in the manner in which he always pays his bill, pre-paid in cash which he sends in an envelope inside the kennel with the dog [*Colm paid his bill with a Platinum MasterCard, earning points towards his frequent flier program*]. Mr. Cope is well-known to me, as over the twenty-eight years of this clinic's operation, I have had the opportunity to treat any number of animals in his care, including guinea pigs, tropical fish, a pair of lovebirds, a ferret named Festus, with a withered leg, all of which have long since died of old age. [*Colm had been to the clinic just a week previously, where Doxie was treated for an ear infection and given a prescription for antibiotics.*] Current patients include his ten-year-old rottweiler registered by the name Fred Flintstone, but which he calls F***face, and the said terrier, approximately four years old, who as far as I know has never been named. Post-procedure, I delivered the terrier to Mr. Cope personally and he accepted it without comment, carrying the terrier into his house in such a way as to suggest the dog had a handle grafted to its back. [*After settling his account, Colm lingered to consult with Dr. Lambert about how best to detoxify Doxie, what diets to follow, and long-term effects; Colm carried her to the car wrapped in a clean blanket, stroking her head, murmuring in her ear.*] Mr. Cope is a difficult, unorthodox sort of personality, but I have no reason to believe his animals are in any way mistreated. I don't believe in de-barking dogs, or in de-clawing cats for that matter, not that Mr. Cope would ever dream of owning a cat, but a pet owner who wants to do these things is well within the law; in this instance, the law even required it of him. [*Dr. Lambert's voice assumed a didactic and scolding tone when he cautioned Colm on the dangers of leaving rodent poison, insect poison or even herbicides where a dog could get at them. "But I don't use those products. We're gardening organically," Colm replied. Dr. Lambert lowered his glasses and peered at Colm over the tops of the wire frames. "You'd keep that stuff out of reach of children, so why not a dog. The dog found it somewhere, Mr."—he picked up the credit card receipt and peered at it for a name—"Simpson." "It's Sinclair," Colm said. "Colm Sinclair."*]

I'll do it if they ask me out of a sense of duty to my patient, who is the animal, and to whom I owe a duty of continuity of care.

◼   ◼   ◼

Zelle @ less than zero
Before Colm and Beverly ever met, they each had few possessions. Colm had:

☐ His 1969 BSA Lightning motorcycle
☐ A trunkful of books
☐ A passport
☐ A set of professional quality cookware
☐ A $25,000 student loan debt in delinquency

Beverly had:

☐ Her Pfaff serger-sewing machine
☐ A wicker trunk full of fabric
☐ Two rolling racks of favourite clothes, some she had designed herself
☐ A passport

When they met at a hostel in Greece, they each had:

☐ A backpack
☐ A money belt
☐ A sunburn

All their other things were in storage in opposite sides of Canada. They spent the next several months travelling through the Greek Islands, Turkey, North Africa. They separated for ten weeks in Morocco, where Beverly took a lover in Essaouira, then another in Marrakesh, and Colm lived in a hotel in Tangiers, smoking opium-laced hashish and imagining conversations with Paul Bowles and William Burroughs. They hooked up again and toured Spain, Portugal and Southern France before they returned to Canada. They parted at Toronto's Pearson International Airport, too tired from the overseas flight to attempt sex in a public place. They had fewer possessions now than when they met, having abandoned:

- ☐ Worn-out clothes
- ☐ Dog-eared guidebooks
- ☐ Most of their money

Beverly made her way home to Goderich on the Georgian Bay, to live with her grandmother. Colm flew on to Calgary, where he crashed on the couches of friends, and rode his motorcycle.

◼ ◼ ◼

Zelle @ 4 months
They never see the old lady, Lydia's mother, Ted's grandmother, until the day the ambulance shows up next door. Then they never see her again. They see Ted's mother Lydia leave her house each morning Tuesday to Saturday at exactly 6:05 a.m. She wears an old-fashioned nurse's cap pinned into her tightly-coiffed silver hair. She covers her starched white uniform with a yellow cardigan, which is replaced as the seasons change in turn by a shapeless grey overcoat with raglan sleeves, then a bulky parka with a fur-lined hood. She is so regular that Colm and Beverly begin to set their own routines by hers. When her old Valiant

turns over and the slant-six valves clatter as she accelerates away, Zelle wakes and starts to cry, unless she is already awake and crying. Colm brings her into their bed, and settles her against Beverly. He has a two-minute shower, and then rummages in the kitchen for coffee. As the months roll by and the baby starts eating solids, he makes Beverly's and Zelle's breakfasts.

"How old do you think she is?" Beverly asks one morning. The three of them are in the darkened living room. Colm hugs his robe closed as he looks out the window. Beverly's been up for an hour, she's pulled on a pair of sweats. Lap-cradled Zelle suckles at one breast, using her free hand to reach through the unbuttoned pyjama top to tweak the other nipple. "She's got to be at least sixty, even sixty-five," Beverly answers her own question. "I mean these houses are over forty years old. Teddy Bear's got to be pushing forty."

They have names for their neighbours. Lydia next door is just Lydia, her son Ted is Teddy Bear. Across the street there's Bill and Betty, who they call the OHITGY's (Ozzie & Harriet In Their Golden Years)—Ricky and David have long since flown the coop, and now Mom and Dad spend their days gardening, golfing, trimming their hedges, sweeping the sidewalks, flashing toothy smiles. Beside them lives Gwyneth, a deaf widow: she's Madame Butterfly, short for social butterfly. Her busy calendar keeps her coming and going all day long. She waves to Colm and Beverly, rocks her arms and gives the thumbs-up to show her appreciation of Zelle. On the other side of the Copes lives Mr. Fish, the Lawnmower Man, a widower who cuts his lawn three times a week and talks to the carp in his fish pond. Around the corner are the Clones, a couple younger than Colm and Beverly, but who are also new to the neighbourhood, have a daughter a few months older than Zelle, who drive the same make and year four-door Toyota as they do. Beverly freaks out the day Mrs. Clone announces she's expecting their second child.

"She looks in good shape," Colm says of Lydia. "Maybe she likes it. You know, keeps fit, sees people. Gives her an excuse to get away from Ted."

"Still," Beverly says.

"Ted." They don't see much of Ted—he hardly ever sets foot outside the house. At the back door with the dogs. Sunday mornings he makes the long trek to the garage in the lane, to fire up his Harley and rev it. They catch a glimpse at the front door when he greets one of the many callers. A daily visit from the Video SuperStore Express (We Deliver!). The pizza guy, Chinese food, dial-a-bottle at all hours of the day or night. Twice a week, the shiny yellow truck with the famous ice cream. The ice cream man comes over the day after Colm and Beverly move in. His name, Artie, is stitched over a breast pocket bristling with pens, a miniature flashlight, and a thermometer.

UPS drivers drop packages at Ted's door. Men on motorcycles come singly or in pairs, or with their old ladies riding on the back. Biker handshakes in greeting. But others too—button-down businessmen, slackers, office temps. College kids, artsy types, silver-haired matrons. These visitors always leave with something—a used plastic grocery bag, bundles wrapped in brown paper and tied with a string. "He's up to something, that bastard. Hydroponics. Methamphetamines. Something."

Every time someone comes to his door, they can hear the terrier start to bark. Zelle starts to cry.

■　　■　　■

Zelle @ 7 months
[From the city website, Animal Services Department: "What to Do When Your Neighbour's Dog Barks"]

Citizens are urged to discuss problems regarding noisy pets directly with the pets' owners before laying a formal complaint with the Animal Services Department. If you can't resolve the dispute, the following outlines the barking dog complaint process:

1. Complainant files a notice with the Animal Services Department.
2. Animal Services notifies the dog owner by mail, with a copy to the complainant. Strict anonymity is preserved by the department.
3. The complainant is also sent a form entitled "Barking Dog Complaint Log" on which to record the instances of barking over a five-day continuous period. THE COMPLAINANT MUST WITNESS THE DOG IN THE ACT OF BARKING ON EACH OCCASION THAT AN ENTRY IS MADE INTO THE LOG. IT IS <u>NOT</u> SUFFICIENT MERELY TO HEAR THE DOG.
4. The complainant forwards the completed log to Animal Services.
5. Animal Services at its discretion may choose to issue a warning or a Notice of Offence.
6. Penalty for first offence is $100, second offence $200, subsequent offences in a 12-month period are $300.

Under the Animal Control Bylaw, the Animal Services

Department has the authority to petition the Provincial Court to declare as a nuisance any animal that is kept within the city limit. Nuisances are defined in the Bylaw, and include but are not limited to noise, mischief, hygiene, destruction of property, perceived menace, etc. The owner of a nuisance animal is subject to maximum penalties of $1,000 in fines per nuisance, imprisonment of 14 days, and seizure and destruction of court-defined nuisance animals in his or her care.

■　　■　　■

Zelle @ almost 9 months
In January, six months after they move in, Colm keeps the Barking Dog Log provided by the city, to document his complaint. It is the second time he has done so. The first time is in November, and he watches, shielded by the curtains, when the Animal Control Officer visits. Beverly refuses to take part, she won't maintain the log when she's at home and Colm's at work. He knows Ted got off with a warning. This time the record-keeping will be unimpeachable. There will be a penalty paid for the sleepless nights, those bark-shattered days.

Beverly has landed a contract sewing costumes for an elaborate production of a Gilbert & Sullivan for the biggest theatre in town. She is working both at home and at the theatre this week. As they move into final fittings and technical rehearsals, she will be away from home full-time. The child-care schedule is complicated, the separation anxiety high. Colm takes a week's vacation to help Beverly with the transition. That week, Colm sees the terrier barking forty-six times, and registers it in the log.

During the show's run, she'll be a dresser; they can pass Zelle off at the door as Beverly dashes for the evening costume call. After Colm's week, for three weeks of rehearsals, Gaddie comes over to "sit." Zelle is almost nine months old. She crawls everywhere, gets stuck under chairs, pulls herself up, knocks over cups. She smiles sometimes. She still cries.

The first day Gaddie cares for Zelle, a chinook blows. The January deep freeze melts away as the temperature soars. When Colm drives up from work, he sees Gaddie towing Zelle in a little penguin-shaped sled he's never laid eyes on. She's standing in the Copes' yard, gesturing a mittened hand as she talks. She's talking to Ted, who has the front screen door with the pheasant decoration propped half-open. He's holding the terrier like a loaf of bread. Zelle is laughing. Laughing. So is Gaddie. Colm slams the car door and marches up the walk into his house without looking over. As he slams the house door for good measure, he hears the dog bark. Zelle's laugh turns to a cry.

"What in hell were you doing out there?" Colm demands of his mother when she comes in with Zelle.

"Oh, Colm, isn't she sweet?" Zelle's wrapped in a tiger-striped snowsuit. Two little ears poke up from the hood. She gurgles.

"Jesus Christ, Mom. I come home and you're practically in his goddamned house."

"Colm. You don't have to use the Lord's name like that." Gaddie slips out of her boots and carries Zelle into the room.

"Jesus Christ Jesus Christ Jesus Christ. It's my own goddamned house, I can say Jesus Christ whenever I damn well please. Jesus Christ."

"I was visiting next door."

"Oh fuck." Zelle's ears perk up. What is that new and interesting word? "With Zelle, I suppose. Are you nuts?"

"Colm, you're overreacting. You let your imagination get away." Gaddie tugs Zelle's arms out of the snowsuit. "I took little ZeeZee for a snow ride—"

"Where did that thing come from?" Colm gestures towards the outside, where the plastic sled sits on the snow of the front yard.

"I picked it up at Sears. Half-price. If you don't like it, I kept the receipt."

"We can't return it now."

"There's hardly a scratch on it. I was out with Zelle, getting her some fresh air. Honestly, I think you two need to get her out of the house more. She's cooped up here all day." She hoists Zelle in her arms. Zelle tugs at her earring and coos.

"Mom, just stop with the teachable moments for once. She gets out all the time."

"If you say so. She was having the time of her life, and we stopped and talked to Lydia. What a delightful woman."

Colm quickly checked out the window: the Valiant was not parked curbside. "Where is she now?"

"Bingo. She asked me to come along. Imagine that. Bingo. In the afternoon. She was just going out, and she asked me for tea some time." She pulls Zelle's fingers away. "Don't do that, dear. That's GaGa's ear. We don't pull on ears." She puts Zelle on a blanket on the floor strewn with rattles and squeaky toys.

"Won't pass that opportunity up, I'm sure. You're here one day and barging in on the neighbours."

"Oh, we didn't really go in."

"Hang on a second, I get it. You were cold-calling her." Colm gets down on the floor and picks up a little yellow star with a ring full of beads attached to it.

"I beg your pardon?"

"You're going to convert her." He rattles the star at Zelle. She rolls towards him and struggles to sit up.

"Well, you're wrong. That wasn't what I was doing at all." Gaddie busies herself collecting her things: her leather-bound phone book, her cellular phone, her slippers. "Besides, Lydia has already accepted Him as our Saviour. She goes to the Celebration Centre downtown. The one in the old theatre. I think it's Pentecost. Or maybe Southern Baptist Convention."

"That makes even more sense. You guys have your own radar."

"Colm, you're impertinent. I noticed the fish bumper sticker on her car."

Zelle has managed to sit up in front of her father. She reaches for the yellow star, and they play tug-of-war. "Lydia invites you to bingo. Okay. Why were you talking to Teddy Bear? Don't tell me he's born again too. Not that fat bastard."

"Really, Colm. Zelle is just enthralled with the little dog."

"Spare me." Colm lets go.

Zelle tips back so her feet go in the air, recovers her balance and settles back down. She giggles, and thrusts the star at Colm. "Did you know he does leatherwork?"

"What are you talking about?"

Gaddie has packed her bag. The zipper of her brightly coloured ski jacket bristles with ski-lift passes. "Edward. He makes things out of leather for people. He's really very talented. People come to him from all over the city."

"You've got to be kidding." Colm tugs at the star again. "I suppose he makes vests for the motorcycle gangs."

"I told him he and Beverly should compare notes. He had no idea she was a tailor." She slips her feet into her fleece-lined boots and zips them up to her ankle.

"She's not a tailor. She's a designer. I don't want him to know anything about us." He pulls on the little star and Zelle leans forward, gripping her end with both hands.

"And he looks after his grandmother."

"What?" Colm has forgotten the three generations next door. He remembers now that Lydia's mother lives with them. "She must be ancient."

"Hmm. She's in her nineties. I didn't meet her. She's bed-ridden."

"Ted looks after her."

"Well, yes. Lydia goes to work every day, so Edward stays home. He works on his leather and looks after his grandmother." Gaddie is standing at the door, bag in one hand, the other on the doorknob. "I've got to get going. Tom and Hazel are coming over and we're going to the IMAX tonight."

"He's an idiot," Colm says. "I pity his grandmother."

Zelle lets go of her side of the rattle. She tips back. Her heels come up. This time she goes over backwards and her head bumps on the blanketed floor. A second's hesitation as she gathers her breath, then she opens her mouth. Her eyes screw shut and tears spring from the corners. She cries.

"Oh, bring her over here so GaGa can kiss her better. My boots are wet, I'll track mud across the room. Colm. Bring her to GaGa. Bring her here." Gaddie holds her arms out.

▪ ▪ ▪

Zelle @ less than zero

Six months after their return to Canada, Beverly shipped herself and her few possessions west on the Greyhound, and moved with Colm and his few possessions into a second floor flat in an old house on Royal Avenue. They purchased the first things that they jointly owned:

☐ A futon that folded into a couch
☐ A console stereo with one working speaker and an 8-track player
☐ A kitchen table with chromium-plated legs and three mismatched chairs with split vinyl seats

Over the next few years, they lived in the basement of a walk-up apartment on Cameron Avenue, shared a house with another couple in Bowness, spent three months travelling in Asia and six more in Australia, where Colm worked as a labourer in a sugar factory and Beverly as a chambermaid in a guesthouse. They got married on a Thursday afternoon on a train platform in a small town on the coast by the Great Barrier Reef. Back in Canada, they house-sat on an acreage near Millarville while Colm commuted by motorcycle to the U of C to complete his engineering degree. They took a one-bedroom in a highrise in the Beltline, then finally an aging rowhouse in Lower Mount Royal. Colm got a job with an international engineering firm. Beverly sewed costumes, bought props, designed, stage managed, ran lights for theatres. Colm still had his motorcycle, in parts now, and his cookware. Beverly had her Pfaff and even more fabric and clothes. They made shelves from chimney bricks and old boards. They had a toaster oven.

■   ■   ■

Zelle @ 6 months
One Sunday in October, Zelle sleeps soundly in the garage. The previous owner has installed a small oscillating fan, barely the width of a person's hand, in the corner of the window facing the house. Its steady hum and slow back-and-forth captivate Zelle and lull her. When Beverly needs a nap, Colm bundles Zelle into her car seat, hauls her to the garage and sets her up on the workbench. Soon her cries subside, replaced by the even breathing of sleep. Colm eventually breaks the spell the fan possesses when he tries to move it into Zelle's nursery. Away from the garage, it fails to soothe her—her fits of crying escalate to face-purpling apoplexy.

Colm opens the overhead door and stands in the lane behind his property. He basks in the autumn sun as it casts its warmth and light onto his upturned face. Above, the clear sky hangs like a blue dome, unmarked by clouds save for the contrail of a jet five miles high. Up and down the lane, behind his neighbours' houses, green and yellow and orange bags full of leaves squat by the gates, ready for the Monday garbage pick up. A squirrel scampers along the overhead wires, its cheeks bulging with forage from bird feeders. Somewhere in the middle distance, a chainsaw whines. Next to his leg, Doxie utters a slow growl in the direction of the squirrel. He pats her head and scratches behind her ear, and the dog lopes back into the garage where she lies down on a scrap of carpet.

Colm hauls out the five-gallon plastic pail full of solvent that he uses as a parts bath and places it in the sunshine out on the driveway. He collects the pieces of the motorcycle transmission from the workbench and drops them into the bucket outside. Sitting on a folding chair, with a pair of heavy black rubber gloves pulled up to his elbows, he cleans the parts, pulling each one from the solvent, scrubbing with an assortment of brushes, scrapers, emery cloth and rags. He lays the cleaned parts out on some cardboard, putting each in its place, so that he constructs an exploded diagram of the final assembly. Where he sits, he can see Zelle as she sleeps. He concentrates on the details of his work, the close scrutiny of cogs and gears for nicks and stress cracks, checking bushings and bearings for wear. He doesn't hear Ted Cope bash his way out the back door, and for once the terrier is quiet.

Colm startles when the Copes' garage door cracks open with a sudden wrenching sound; the chain on the opener chatters as it lifts. The smell of marijuana drifts into the afternoon. Colm checks Zelle—she stirs, then stills. Doxie lifts her head and watches Colm. Ted Cope saunters out of his garage. He is well over six feet. His gut protrudes, as big and solid as a granite boulder. He is barefoot, and his yellow toenails look like talons. In lieu of pants, he sports a pair of Bermuda shorts cut from a fabric that looks like the burlap of coffee sacks. His shirt is a red and black-checked lumberjack number. His uncombed hair hangs in hanks past his shoulders, no ponytail today. He holds the terrier under one arm, and appears to be feeding it a foot-long frozen frankfurter. He looks over at Colm and nods.

"Howdy neighbour," he says. Colm stands up. He is holding

the spline in his rubber-gloved hand. "Hi," he replies. Colm and Beverly have been in their house four or five months. This is the first conversation either of them has had with Ted. He looks at the motorcycle part Colm holds, takes in the clean parts on the cardboard. "You got a bike," he says.

"Yes," Colm replies. "BSA Lightning. Time for a rebuild. Again."

"British hog," Ted says, and snorts as if half in laughter and half in contempt. "Got an old '47 hardtail. Knucklehead." He nods his head towards his garage. "Restored her from the ground up."

"Really," Colm says. He has been curious about the rumble of the v-twin on Sunday afternoons. "Can I have a look?"

"Knock yourself out." Ted takes another stick of meat from the pocket of his shorts and pokes it into the snout of the dog in his arms. "Man, this guy loves his frozen wieners. Puppy popsicles." Doxie trots out and stands by Colm, licking her lips as she watches the little dog. The terrier stops long enough to stare back at Doxie and give a sharp bark of warning. Then it resumes eating. Colm checks Zelle to ensure she is still asleep, then walks over to the other garage.

Amid the clutter—45-gallon drums, piles of unidentifiable vehicle parts, a stack of what appears to be animal hides, a greasy couch, boxes of canning jars, several lawn mowers, the hood of a truck set on blocks to serve as a table of sorts—the motorcycle shines like a polished gem. The Knucklehead motor pancakes the classic Harley-Davidson twin-v engine design, but it looks anything but old. The bike gleams, glossy black, deep blue enamel and chrome. The big stainless coil springs under the saddle offer the only rear suspension. The saddle itself is a work of art. Black leather as polished as a cadet's boots. Leatherwork around the rim of the seat etched in a pattern of Celtic rings. A pair of hand-tooled saddlebags straddling the rear fender shows a relief of interlocking vines and roses. The rivets in the saddle and the bags have the lustre of sterling silver. The mahogany knob on the suicide hand-shifter is burnished with the patina of both wear and care. A classic piece of motorcycle history, not chopped or channelled Easy Rider-style, but customized to preserve the lines of the original design.

"Jesus. This is fantastic," Colm says. "You did all this work?"

Ted doesn't look up, just shrugs as he feeds his dog. "It's fuck-all."

"Hardly. This belongs in a museum. An art gallery." Colm notices a couple of Sturgis Hill Climb posters from the early eighties on the back of a red mechanic's tool box. There's an old movie poster of Marlon Brando from *The Wild One*. Someone has traced a moustache and a soul patch on his face with a grease pencil, and added a cartoon caption, so he seems to be saying: Live Free or Die. "I can imagine Lee Marvin or Brando hopping on this thing and driving away."

"Hmph," Ted grunts. "Not Brando, he was on English iron. Triumph T-bird. Marvin rode the HD. Brando was such a fucking wuss."

"Do you ride much?" Colm asks. He really wants to ask: Do you know British bikes?

"Nah. Not anymore. My last steady ride was a Sportster. Some people think that's a ladies' bike, but man, that was a fast piece of work. I just built this one for fun."

"Can I sit on it?"

"Like the man said, knock yourself out." Colm swings his leg over and eases it off the kickstand. "It's heavy," he says. "Solid. Wow. Wide." He pulls the front brake hand lever, slides his foot into the floorboards and toes the clutch, fingers the suicide stick. "It's like driving a car. It's weird having only one handlebar lever."

"I'll find you a brain bucket, you can take it for a spin."

"No. I mean I'd love to, but I got my baby in the garage."

"Baby," Ted says. "Suit yourself." The dog licks his fingers, sniffs around his person for more. "That's it. You've had enough, ya little porker."

"Pardon," Colm says.

"Talking to the runt here." He puts the dog down. Immediately it races over to Colm, snorts around his shoes, then starts to bark. It lunges towards Doxie, who stands by the open door. She backs off a couple of steps. Her tail wags, then stops. She sets her head at an angle.

Colm dismounts and looks down at Ted's dog: "It's okay, Doxie won't bite you," he says to the terrier.

Ted laughs. "Yeah right. You could hit that little furball with a hammer and he wouldn't back down." The terrier bares its teeth and advances. Doxie retreats across the property line and into her own garage. The dog turns and snaps its jaws at Colm.

Colm hears Zelle now, awake, responding to the barking with cries of her own. "Man, your dog barks all the time," Colm says.

"Like your kid," Ted says.

"Pardon?"

Ted shrugs. "My dog barks. Your kid cries. Same difference."

"Hardly the same, I think," Colm says.

"Sure it is. Calling for attention. Just different species. It's in their nature."

"No, it's different. A child isn't some species. She's a person. She cries when she needs something."

"Whatever, man. All's I'm saying is, doesn't all that whining get under your skin? Does that brat ever shut up?" The dog runs in circles now, barking, barking, barking.

"What did you say?" Colm is at the door, his body angled towards his own place and to the sounds of his daughter, but he hesitates.

"You heard me. Or is that the problem? The rugrat cries and you're deaf to it."

"I've got to go see my child."

"Yeah. Go. Put a plug in it while you're at it."

Colm picks up Zelle from her seat and rocks her against him. Next door the Knucklehead Harley roars to life. The throbbing twin-v, barely muffled, echoes through the lane and the windows rattle. Zelle cries even harder, and Colm can hear Doxie join in the barking as he rushes to the house.

◼   ◼   ◼

Zelle @ 3 weeks

"I never thought I'd own a house."

"I never thought I'd want to own a house."

"Do you?"

"What?"

"Want to own? Are we making a mistake?"

"Yes. No. This is what we talked about. A safe place for our family."

"Roots. Stability."

"Better than paying rent."

"We're not paying rent now."

"Zelle can't grow up at her grandmother's. Neither can we."

"We need our space."

"It's so final. A commitment."

"And Zelle's not?"

"It's not the same thing. A house is not a baby. We'll never just be able to pick up and go. We used to pick up and go places."

"You used to do that."

"You too."

"Buying a house seems like a failure somehow."

"A failure of what?"

"Ideas. Conviction. Ideals. A sell-out of ideals."

"So now you're a revolutionary?"

"I guess so."

"We talked about this. We wanted a garden and flowers and a place for Zelle and Doxie to play and an outdoor shower. We need to figure a way we can walk around nude in the backyard so nobody sees."

"I just thought I'd never be one of those people. I hated those people."

"Who?"

"The bad people. People who own things. People who want to abolish Medicare and ban books. People who never read books. People in motorhomes towing sport utility vehicles with boats on top. People who care about lawn fertilizer."

156

"Wow."

"Those people all own houses."

"We're not those people. I'm not those people."

"I hope so."

◼   ◼   ◼

Zelle @ 10 weeks
[*The Ice Cream Man speaks*]
I bring Ted ice cream Tuesdays and Fridays, but I never make new customer visits on Fridays, so it's a Tuesday. I've been delivering to Ted for years. So I know it's gotta be a Tuesday the first time I ring their bell. They've just moved in. The house next door is exactly the same as Ted's, it was his uncle's or something. I've seen the For Sale sign, so I'm hopeful. New people. New customers.

So this one day, a Tuesday like I said, I'm bringing Ted his ice cream. I bring him two buckets a week—he likes it twice. Vanilla every Tuesday, and that's when he orders whatever for Friday. Chocolate Crunch, Butterscotch, Spumoni, Pralines'n'Cream. I never know what he's going to come up with. I tried to get him once to go for a single delivery, saves me a trip, but he insists. Hey, the customer's always right.

His dog is going nuts as usual. He yells at his dog. His dog just barks. It's so excited it's like it's gonna explode. That dog's gotta learn how to relax or it's a goner. Ted tells me they moved in next door.

So I go back to my truck, get my clipboard, a few flyers. Everybody thinks of us, the big yellow trucks, they think ice cream, but we do more than ice cream. Steaks, chicken cordon blue, cheesecake. We've even got those cocktail sausages for parties. Eggs. Frozen omelettes. Stick 'em in the microwave, instant breakfast. Ted tells me they're a young couple, a kid that's always bawling. Perfect customers, I think. These people need me. I check myself in the outside rearview, make sure I don't have any spinach stuck in my teeth. My uniform's clean, it's a good uniform we've got. Like something a milkman would wear in one of those old *Saturday Evening Post* magazines. People like it. I've got my pens and thermometer and flashlight nicely arranged in my pocket. I'm ready.

I go up to the house. They've got a sheet or blanket tacked up half-assed over the window, but I figure, whatever, they just moved in. I ring the doorbell. Right away a baby starts howling. This guy answers the door, he's got the baby kind of tucked under his arm. Like he's holding a football with arms and legs hanging down on either side of his forearm. This kid's head is in the crook of his elbow, and crying. I mean, wailing. I can hear Ted's dog through the wall next door start barking again. This kid's face is purple with crying. The guy's rubbing the kid's back, as if that's gonna help.

"Hi," I go. "Nice kid. He's just a wee one." I crouch to get a better look, not that I really care, but I know you gotta pay attention to the babies. "You gotta great voice, kiddo," I say. "You're gonna be a regular Pavarotti."

"He's a she," the guy says.

"Well, that's just great," I say. I can see behind him into the living room. It's gloomy in there. They've got one of those Japanese mattress things in the middle of the floor, and there's this lady flat on her back, she's got her arms flung back over her head and her kimono thing rides up almost to her hoo-hoo. She's got her eyes wide open, but she never looks over at me, never hardly moves. She's just looking up at the ceiling. There's a bunch of boxes all over the place and two lawn chairs and an old TV with rabbit ears set up on a milk crate.

I try to keep from staring at the lady, so I launch into my pitch: Just making a delivery to a valued customer next door, saw a new neighbour, thought I'd check to see if you needed anything, blah, blah, blah. "We do a lot more than ice cream." The guy cuts me off.

"Did I ask you here?" he goes.

"Pardon me," I say.

"You heard me. I didn't ask you here, so go away." And he shuts the door, just like that. I mean, what a jerk. You need a tough skin for this racket, and don't get me wrong, this guy didn't even register on my radar. I get nine doors shut in my face for every new customer I sign, but this guy. I can hear his kid howling all the way back to the truck, and Ted's dog is still barking his way to a freaking coronary too.

Next time I'm at Ted's I notice there's a sign by the guy's door, and I check it out. It's taped right over the doorbell, it says:

DO NOT RING OR KNOCK

BABY SLEEPING

GO AWAY

I can hear the kid screaming. Sleeping my ass. That note's still there. I mean, it's just something I check, I take a mental note of. I hear from Ted all the grief he's going through with the guy over his dog and whatever, and he's still got this sign: GO AWAY.

■ ■ ■

Zelle @ 10 months

Beverly and Colm start having sex again. Zelle stops crying for the most part, except when she is wakened in the night. Beverly spends the day with Zelle, Colm rushes home from work each afternoon. They have a half-hour before Beverly goes to the theatre for the show call. Zelle crawls back and forth between them as Beverly sits in the rocking chair in the kitchen expressing breast milk for a bedtime snack. Colm busies himself at the counter, mashing organic avocados, peas and cottage cheese, baking yams in the microwave for Zelle's supper. Zelle laughs and laughs. She pulls herself up on Daddy's leg. She bangs on pots and pans. She gabbles in her own language. She tastes the things she finds on the floor.

Beverly shakes the last drops of breast milk through the diaphragm of the pump. She caps the collection bottle and puts it in the fridge. "Just put the pump in the sink and I'll boil it out after Zelle goes to bed," Colm says.

"You're such a mensch." Beverly picks up Zelle and swings her in the air. "Who's my favourite baby?" she says, "Who's my favourite baby?" Zelle howls with delight.

"Working the baby angle," Colm says.

"Group hug," and the three of them come together, Zelle pressed between Mom and Dad. "Let's have another one of these," Beverly says.

"A whole baseball team."

"No, really. Let's have another one soon. We're not getting younger."

"We're barely surviving this one." Zelle makes a grab at Colm's glasses. He turns his head and she gets a fistful of hair. "Ouch. Gentle, baby. Be gentle." Zelle loosens her grip and pats his head. "See, she's learning." He looks at Beverly. "It means we'll have to have sex."

"Ooh, ick. Will I have to kiss you?"

She kisses him, playfully, then again, a longer deeper one.

"Wow. Okay." Zelle laughs and reaches over to tug at her mom's lip.

She comes home from the theatre after eleven, and for four nights running they make love.

"Hey, you're good at this. Have you been practising?"

"Just on my own."

"On your own! You devil. Seed spiller."

"You're not so bad yourself."

"Like riding a bicycle."

Exhausted by their days, their nights, themselves, they pillow-talk each other to sleep.

"She's so amazing."

"We haven't wrecked her. Yet."

"What do you mean?"

"She's still so pure."

"How do other people do it?"

"Do what?"

"It. This. Have five kids. Work three jobs each. Keep a neat home. Throw dinner parties. Restore antiques. Embroider doilies. Keep the grass cut. Shovel the walks. Balance their chequebook. Volunteer for the Food Bank. Lobby for world peace."

"Hush up and ravish me."

On the fifth night, Colm has just finished tasting the sweet milk from Beverly's nipple ("Is that a turn-on?" "Just an occupational hazard.") and is tracing a line of kisses down her breastbone and over her navel when the dog starts to bark.

"Damn," Colm says. His shoulders stiffen and he lifts his head.

"Ignore it, Colm."

"That damn dog." He can hear Doxie in the kitchen as she stirs and returns a soft growl back to the neighbour's terrier. The dog barks.

"For god's sake, Colm, let it go." She reaches for him, but he pulls free.

"He does it on purpose. It's one o'clock in the bloody morning and he does it on purpose. Listen to that. He's egging it on." Along with the barking of the terrier they can hear Ted's voice as he yells at Fuckface, the rottweiler. Colm pulls on a robe and storms out of the bedroom into the small den that serves as an office. He finds a form titled Barking Dog Complaint Log, grabs a pen and goes to the window that faces the neighbour's yard.

▣　　▣　　▣

Zelle @ 0 to three months
When Beverly was pregnant, they moved into Gaddie's condo while she went to Africa on a mission. They sold or gave away all their stuff, and concentrated on erasing their debts. While Gaddie was away, they acquired:

　□ A two-year-old chocolate-brown Labrador retriever,
　　 Doxie, whose breeder-owners had concluded she did

not conform; Doxie was purchased as protection for Beverly after she let a man into the condo
- ☐ A five-year-old Toyota four-door sedan with low mileage
- ☐ A line of credit

Three weeks after Zelle was born, they closed the deal on the bungalow, but didn't take possession until she was two-and-a-half months old. The house came equipped with:

- ☐ A garage with door opener
- ☐ Seven appliances and a gas barbecue

Before they moved in, Colm scrubbed and painted the smallest bedroom for Zelle, then repainted one wall because Beverly insisted it needed a complementary colour opposite the window. When he was done, Colm acknowledged that she was right. As a house-warming gift, Gaddie equipped the nursery:

- ☐ A crib with Winnie-the-Pooh decorations, and a matching chest of drawers full of clothes
- ☐ A specialized no-fuss no-smell diaper pail
- ☐ A Winnie-the-Pooh mobile to hang over the crib

◼   ◼   ◼

Zelle @ 13 months

Over three months, Colm maintains a continual Barking Dog Log. Every Monday, he phones the Animal Services Bylaw Enforcement to lay his complaint. The visits by the dogcatcher become part of the routine of the neighbourhood.

KNUCKLEHEAD & OTHER STORIES

The barking gets worse. Ted goes out into the yard at all hours, plays fetch with a glow-in-the-dark mini-Frisbee. The terrier's yapping incites Doxie to growl and whine. Zelle cries in the night.

By the middle of May, the bylaw enforcement officer has taken to parking a couple of houses up the street between his dispatches. Colm watches from the front window as he delivers yet another ticket to Ted. "He must owe thousands in fines."

"I wish you'd just drop it."

"Ma-ma-ma-ma-ma," Zelle says. She cruises from couch to table to chair, walking but hanging on to the furniture. She stops. A jack-in-the-box with a cock-a-doodling rooster is in the middle of the floor. She lets go of the chair and stands, reaching both hands to the rooster. "Ma-ma-ma."

"Too bad they just can't seize the dog." He had researched the bylaw on the Internet.

"Really, Colm. You've been over this and over this." Beverly watches Zelle. She puts one foot forward, then draws it back. "Your daughter's about to take her first steps. Shouldn't you have a video camera or something?"

Colm glances over from where he's standing by the curtain just as Zelle makes a decision. She falls back on her bum, scoots onto all fours, then crawls over to the rooster. "Ma-ma-ma-ma."

"He'll never pay the fines. That's the thing. He'll ignore it and just keep whipping that dog into a frenzy."

"So why bother." Beverly crouches down, and stuffs the rooster back in the box. Zelle fingers the button that activates it. "A little harder, Zelle."

"Ma-ma-ma," Zelle says. She pokes at the toy, and the rooster pops up.

◼ ◼ ◼

Zelle @ 9 months
[Gaddie's Lament]
You dropped Zelle. You didn't drop her, she fell out of her high-chair. Beverly yells at you and you want to slap her face. You've never slapped a face in your life, never hit anyone, never spanked Colm as a boy, but you want to slap her face. You imagine the sting in the palm of your hand, the red outlines of your long slim fingers rising on her cheek. You know you did up the safety strap. Did you hear it snap closed? Beverly demands of you. You want to slap her. You turned your back for only a few seconds, you knew the strap was done up. Was it tight? You wonder if Zelle managed to undo it. There was a two-year-old boy in Utah who undid his car seat buckle and wandered away into the woods to freeze to death. Zelle's only nine months old, she can't even pick up her own food, for christ's sake, Beverly says. She takes the Lord's name in vain. Both of them. Their deliberate blasphemy.

It would never have happened, you say, it would never have happened if you hadn't had to scrub the highchair tray. You had to take the tray across the kitchen to scrub away its filth. Zelle was in the chair, but then you saw the crusted porridge, the smeared avocado, the gluey banana bits. You wouldn't serve your granddaughter on such a filthy tray. Your granddaughter deserves better. It would never have happened if. Does it ever get washed? You are too old, you think, to be cleaning house for your lazy godless daughter-in-law and your feckless son. Not too old physically. You are able to walk to great distances, carry heavy burdens, bear privation and austerity. You proved that in

Africa on your mission. But for this. Why does she insist on going to work? Why does Colm allow it? The most important job she has is here, at home, with her child, with your granddaughter. You stayed home. Even after Alec died, you stayed home. You ask now if they have life insurance and they scoff at you. You could tell them. The tray was filthy. Zelle is fine, babies are resilient, you say. But you called Beverly anyway. You called and she left the rehearsal hall and now she says she'll never get another contract with that theatre and it's your fault because Zelle fell out of the highchair. Are you happy? Isn't this what you wanted? A stay-at-home daughter-in-law?

Beverly goes back to work and you move the fridge and stove and sweep up the dust bunnies and dried elbow macaroni and shrivelled peas and toast crusts and hardened bits of orange peel. You put Zelle in her crib where she's perfectly safe and let her cry and cry and cry and cry, but in twenty minutes or a half an hour she's asleep and she sleeps and sleeps, and you clean behind the fridge and stove and save the sweepings in the dustpan on the counter to show Colm when he comes home from work. Look what was behind the stove. And Zelle wakes and she cries, but you finish the last of four loads of laundry, folding the clothes and towels into towering stacks on their queen-size bed. You pick up, you dust, you chop vegetables for supper. When Colm comes home, the house is neat and clean and smelling of onions and the laundry is clean and piled high on the bed, and the dustpan of sweepings is on the counter. You say nothing, you hold Zelle, quiet and smiling in your arms, you say nothing, let the home speak for itself.

Zelle cries in her crib, but she hushes as soon you hold her.

She coos and giggles and settles for you like she does for no one else. The grandma factor, Colm says. She fusses and cries, but she settles for you. So different from Colm as a baby. But the same too, the same wonder of the little life in your arms. You can get lost staring at a baby's face. Alec loved to watch Colm sleep. Zelle looks like her grandfather in her eyes and her little ears. Your husband had the smallest, cutest ears, perfect shells with hardly any lobe. Zelle has his ears, you can stare at them as Zelle coos in your arms. Colm was a calm baby, so small, smaller than Zelle ever was. A wee bairn, not even five pounds, they wanted him in the incubator but you pleaded, and old Dr. Williams showed up at last smelling like whisky and pipe tobacco, he missed the delivery, and he said, Oh, he's a fine healthy lad, he just needs his mom. So Colm stayed with you in your ward, the nurses cluck-clucked, it was out of the ordinary in those days, but Alec's insurance covered a private ward, this was before Medicare, you had your own insurance then. Dr. Williams was so old-fashioned, he even delivered babies at home, he'd be right up-to-date today. He did insist that bottle-feeding was best for a baby, especially a small one like Colm, so those first few days in your private ward, you held Colm in your lap and let him suck from the easy-flowing rubber nipple of a glass bottle. When your milk let down, the nurses bound your breasts with a wide elastic bandage—oh how they ached, a burning throbbing ache— but after a day or two you stopped leaking milk every time Colm cried and the ache went away.

Beverly and Colm insist on breastfeeding Zelle. Those first few weeks they stayed with you at your condo before they moved into this house, Zelle crying and crying, Beverly in tears.

Colm blocked the doorway while you tried to enter the room with a bottle. He was always so stubborn. All of them. They made their choice and would not listen to your reason. Sometimes mother does know best, you would say. Beverly was mad. Angry and unreasonable. Her nipples cracked and bleeding, she forced her breast into tiny Zelle's crying mouth. Colm hovered over them both, mother and child, trying to offer advice, getting his own hands in there to help, until Beverly would explode and push him away and run to the bathroom where she would lock herself in with Zelle.

The dog next door starts barking, and a car with a loud muffler roars to life in the street. You hear the profane voices of men hollering gruff goodwill to each other. The dog barks. You warned them about this neighbourhood. It's old, it's second generation, no kids, bad schools. Indians from the Sarcee reserve are bussed in and cause trouble. One of the women in your ladies' auxiliary at the church works for the school board, you know the trouble spots. Beverly always corrects you when you say Indian: First Nations, she says, and they call themselves Tsuu T'ina. You warned them about this neighbourhood. It is beneath their potential. Full of old people who can't keep up their houses. Men who run plumbing and heating businesses from their garages. Revenue properties rented out to who-knows-what. You hear their neighbour's dog barking and Zelle stirs. She spits out the nipple of the bottle of expressed breast milk you are feeding her. Her bright blue eyes are wide, beseeching you. There, there, you say, rocking her gently. You sing her a song. Jesus loves you, this I know. The dog barks again and Zelle squirms and sets up her crying. You take her to show her the dog through the side window. There's the doggie, you say. The happy terrier runs to and fro in the back yard on the other side of the chain-link fence. The man stands in full view, smoking. He is unkempt and unruly, swearing at the terrier and another big dog who does not bark. You wave to him when he looks your way, and you lift crying Zelle's hand and wave it too. You do not like the look of this man, but you believe in the Christian responsibility to be kind to your neighbours. You are ashamed too of Colm and his behaviour, the escalation of bylaws and enforcement officers and community mediation with strangers over a barking dog. It is unneighbourly and ungodly. How is this man Colm such a stranger to you now, when Colm the baby was your world?

Sometimes Colm would let you take him in your arms, an unfamiliar embrace, when Beverly locked herself and Zelle in the bathroom of your condo. You would lead him downstairs and tell him stories of how he was so small as a baby, and how you fed him bottle after bottle he was such a greedy gus, and you would get him to admit that formula might not be such a bad idea. But Beverly refused to consider it, and Colm always fell under her sway, and then he would block the doorway, refusing you, his mother, near. They haven't seen the babies you have seen starving to death in Africa on mother's milk. They haven't witnessed the miracles that you have—that after two days on formula the African babies have a glow you can see even through their black skin, the hollowness in their eyes gives way to the unmistakable signs of spirit. They haven't seen what you have. And look at Colm, a formula baby. Beverly too, you suspect.

■ ■ ■

Zelle @ 15 months

Colm's dog is sick. He goes to the back yard and calls, "Doxie! Doxie!" He has a bowl of canned dog food in one hand, and a horse pill in his pocket that he needs to get her to swallow. She doesn't come to his calling. "Doxie, c'mon girl." There aren't many places a dog the size of Doxie could hide in the back yard.

Colm checks the long, narrow space between the garage and the fence. He looks under the skirt of the blue spruce by the back gate. "Doxie-kins. Dr. Ballard's special treat." Canned dog food is a sick-dog meal. She isn't by the composter either, but he almost slips and falls when he steps in a fresh runny stool. In that corner of the yard, near the vegetable patch, the lawn is freckled with yellow-green splashes of Doxie's diarrhoea. "Damn," Colm says. "Doxie! Doxie!"

At that moment, Ted seems to kick his way out of his house. He has one arm wrapped around an enormous stainless steel bowl that is mounded high with what looks like popcorn topped with gravy. In his other hand, he grips the Yorkshire terrier.

The sleeves of Ted's black AC/DC t-shirt have been ripped or hacked away, exposing beefy arms dotted with blue smudges of tattoos. His green sweat pants are greasy and stained. Grey jockey shorts peek through a collection of holes just to one side of his crotch, suggesting a long-ago accident with battery acid. Yellow bedroom slippers are wedged over his feet. His long hair, shot through with grey, is gathered in a loose ponytail. The whiskers of his thick beard have been gathered into braids, like dreadlocks on his chin. The small dog squirms in the man's encyclopedia-sized hand, emitting a breathy sound like an orchestra of cats coughing up hairballs.

A chain rattles on the neighbour's patio as the other dog, the rottweiler the size of a small pony, cautiously emerges from a collection of lumber, a lean-to-like kennel of boards piled against the side of the house. He slinks towards the man, the stump of his tail and anvil-shaped head kept low. "C'mere, Fuckface," Ted says to the big dog. He puts the bowl down. "Here's your fucking snack." Ted eats a couple of handfuls—it *is* popcorn covered in gravy—then offers some to the snuffling terrier clenched in his fist. The small dog slurps up the food, then hisses and snaps in the direction of the rottweiler. Fuckface hesitates, then inches forward. He slurps up the food in a few gulps, and then licks the bowl clean, keeping his eyes on the terrier.

Colm tries not to look. "Doxie?" he calls. He checks the gate latch and the door to the garage to make sure they're shut tight. He's aware that his neighbour is watching him, and he can hear the other man laughing with a slow chuckle, "Heh-heh-heh." Colm ignores it. Ted leans on the low chain-link fence between the two yards, laughing harder. The terrier gasps in his arms.

Colm swings towards him. "What exactly is so funny?" He is much closer than he would ever wish to be. If he'd hold out the dog dish in his hand, the terrier would eat the food.

"I can see your shit-eatin' Doxie," Ted says. "And she's not looking so hot. Heh-heh-heh." Colm looks where he is looking, and sees a single paw protruding from underneath his deck. "Doxie!" he says with alarm. There doesn't seem to be enough room for a Labrador retriever in that narrow space. He scrambles to his hands and knees; with difficulty he pulls Doxie from her hiding place. Her chocolate-brown fur is matted with feces. Her eyes are half-open and glazed. Frothy drool hangs from her slack jaw. Colm puts his ear to her chest cavity. Her heartbeat is racing and irregular.

Ted still snickers, and his dog barks silently and madly. Colm turns on him. "Stop that! She might be dying." He picks up Doxie, who makes an awkward bundle in his arms. "Doxie, girl, it's all right. We'll get help."

The neighbour hawks and spits into Colm's peonies. "It'll serve you right if your fucking dog croaks." He smashes his way back into the house.

◼   ◼   ◼

Zelle @ 12 months
[The Dogcatcher's Soliloquy]
I am not the most popular person to appear on your doorstep. I am in league with those workers who are almost universally despised—the meter maid, the traffic cop, the clerk at the vehicle impound lot, the tow truck driver, the bill collector, the tax assessor, the security guard at the airport gate, the clerk at the unemployment office, the customs officer. We are the low-level functionaries of the bureaucracy who are inevitably the source of your grief. If we don't cost you money, we cost you time. And we try your patience. If there is a positive result from your encounter with us (you get your automobile back, your unemployment cheque is issued), it is only achieved through hardship (your car was towed, you lost your job). I know only

too well the bittersweet reaction engendered by my presence at your door.

I still call myself a dogcatcher, though my title is Animal Services Bylaw Enforcement Officer. But "dogcatcher" has an old-timey feel to it, like "chimneysweep" or "fishmonger." When I think of myself as a dogcatcher, I can place myself in a tradition—my professional forebears helped keep the streets safe from rabid mongrels, protected children from packs of wild dogs. There was likely a dogcatcher in attendance when Socrates drank his hemlock (or perhaps on the tribunal that condemned him). I can imagine a dogcatcher in a Charles Dickens novel, during the plague of London in 1666, in Roman times. I'm surprised there is no "Dogcatcher's Tale" in Chaucer.

Mirabile dictu, the dispute between Mr. Cope and Mr. Sinclair is not the most extreme to which I have been a party. I say "a party to," because, alas, the dogcatcher is never a neutral player in these dramas. My part is usually that of the intermediary agent who holds the power, but who stands aside of the central conflict— Creon to Oedipus, Virgil to Dante, Merlin to Arthur, Tashtego to Ahab. As agent of the complainant, the dogcatcher does the duty of avenger, more often than not taking possession of someone's cherished pet; as the unwelcome messenger, the dogcatcher makes parley with the offending party, offering the terms and conditions for the return of the captive. Emotions can run high, and not infrequently these emotions are directed at me. I vividly recall the vicious dog court hearing at which I testified, where the judgment went against the owner. He went berserk—he threatened me, he threatened the neighbour whose Pekingese had been killed, and whose son had been bitten and required forty-two stitches in the face. He threatened the judge, he threatened the court bailiffs. His was the rage of Achilles who would challenge the very gods. The case of Sinclair v. Cope was mild indeed.

For one thing, Mr. Cope never attempted to lay a counter-claim. In a barking dog dispute, particularly after multiple citations, the defendant usually turns the tables. I know Mr. Sinclair has his own dog, a fine-looking Lab, but it was never the object of my duty. Both men, while harbouring obvious antipathy towards the other, remained civil. When I suggested to Mr. Sinclair, as is our policy, that the two could engage (free-of-charge) the services of a community negotiator trained in conflict resolution, he was polite but firm: "I don't speak with Mr. Cope. This is not a point for negotiation. His dog is a nuisance." Mr. Cope's response was equally blunt: "I don't like to go out of my house," he said. "And what's to talk about? My neighbour's a jerk, he harasses me, I could sue his ass. But I've got a thick skin. Like Shakespeare said, Is not a terrier a dog? And does not a dog bark?"

On the one hand, I sympathized with Mr. Cope—I issued a total of ten notices with fines and three warnings in a period of barely seven months. (Not that Mr. Cope ever made any effort to pay his penalties.) Yet I understood Mr. Sinclair's position too—the law puts the duty of controlling a dog to its owner, and the same law allows for citizen complaints, the levy of penalties and the intervention of the court. And I must add that I never attended Mr. Cope's home when his dog was not barking.

In the end, it was only when I fulfilled the destiny of my role that the situation escalated beyond the limits of civility. Having determined that Mr. Cope owed $2,700 in fines, having heard from his own lips that he had no intention of changing his or his dog's behaviour, having witnessed the dog and its never-ceasing barking, having consulted the Animal Services Department's Policies & Procedures, having discussed and documented the matter with my supervisor, I recommended that the matter be brought before the court and the dog be declared a nuisance dog. The law allows for this. By a quirk of the legislation, it does not allow for the entry to the owner's premises and seizure of a nuisance dog as it does for a dangerous dog. First we must catch it running at large. But I knew that was inevitable. It is what I do. I catch dogs.

◼ ◼ ◼

Zelle @ 3 to 8 months

They spent several Saturdays arguing their way through furniture stores. Eventually, piece by piece, they bought:

☐ A queen-size bed with an arts and crafts headboard
☐ A refectory table at an auction
☐ An antique sideboard at an estate sale

They couldn't decide on a couch. As the months rolled by, they began to leaf through the flyers that arrived in their mailbox every Wednesday and Sunday. They found they needed:

☐ A lawnmower, hedge clippers, rakes, shovels, hoes, spades, garden forks, peat moss, manure, soil in plastic bags, a hammer, a drill, a saw, a tool box
☐ A coffee maker

Beverly made regular trips to children's stores:

☐ A stroller
☐ Toys, books for babies, and books for parents about their babies
☐ A nursing bra
☐ A different nursing bra
☐ A baby monitor

By the time Zelle was eight months old, they decided that Beverly should try to take on some work, even temporary or part-time, so they could reduce the balance on their line of credit and keep current with their credit cards. Beverly went out and bought:

☐ A breast pump
☐ A different breast pump

◼ ◼ ◼

Zelle @ 13 months
It is a Friday. Colm is sick with a summer cold, working at home. He's got his laptop spread out on the refectory table in the dining room, working on a set of engineering specifications for a new computer science building at the university. Still in his bathrobe at two in the afternoon. Beverly and Zelle have gone to meet Colm's mother Gaddie for a picnic in Heritage Park and a ride on the steam train. Zelle loves trains. Doxie lies curled at his feet, twitching her ears and forefeet in her dog dreams.

The wail of sirens pricks his consciousness as they approach. Usually they slide by on Heritage Drive a few blocks over, dopplering in and out of range. But these zero in, he can hear the roar of the diesels on the trucks. Doxie pops her head up. When she rises and pads to the window, Colm follows. The Fire Department Emergency Response Unit is the first to pull up, almost parking on his lawn. An ambulance arrives from the other direction and stops in the street in front of the Copes'. Colm notices the Animal Services truck two doors down, parked where it has often been over the last month. Another fire truck and a police car arrive.

He counts two paramedics, three firefighters and a police officer who enter the house. Another five firefighters and a police officer stand around their vehicles, talking among themselves, leaning their ears to the radio receivers pinned to their epaulets. Colm moves out to the front porch to eavesdrop. Lydia pulls up in her battered Valiant and parks facing the wrong way in front of Gwyneth's. She rushes inside.

The police officer and two of the firefighters bustle out of the house. They retrieve the gurney from the ambulance and wheel it back inside. Then they come back into the street. There is a brief huddle, then the fire vehicles and the police car drive away. From the porch, Colm can see Gwyneth at her window, the sheers pulled aside. Betty has come to the front of her yard across the street, and kneels facing the Copes' on a little pad while she stabs a small garden fork into a flower bed. Mr. Fish has turned off his lawnmower, and stands on the sidewalk, hands on his hips, attention focussed on the ambulance. Everyone waits.

A few minutes later, the paramedics and the firefighter appear, manoeuvring the stretcher through the front door. It is the only time Colm lays eyes on Ted's grandmother. The image that he keeps, that he will use to describe her to Beverly, is that of a pile of dry white leaves. She is awake, conscious, and as they struggle to lift her down the steps, a wafer-like hand floats up from the sheet draped over her to pull the oxygen mask down over her chin. Her lips are a pucker of thin blue lines, moving rapidly, without sound. The firefighter is holding an IV bag over her head, and as the response team sets the stretcher down on the sidewalk, he uses his other hand to try to put the mask back in place over her mouth. She tosses her head, and Colm can see the elastic snap down over her ear. The hand tethered to the IV brushes at the air.

Ted storms out of the house. "What the fuck are you doing! She doesn't want that on her face. Fuck, stupid." Ted is shirtless, with a pair of dirty blue jeans hanging off his butt. He's got that dog in his fist like a ham sandwich, and the dog is barking. "She's trying to talk. She wants to tell me something." Ted pushes his way to his grandmother's side. He drops the dog, and it scampers away.

Ted gathers the old woman's hands into his and leans close to her lips. Colm can see she stops trying to speak, and her eyes lock on to Ted's. She seems to relax. "It's okay, Gamma," Ted says softly. "Momsy'll go with you." He strokes the wisps of hair aside as the paramedic replaces the mask and the firefighter checks the IV. Ted stands aside as they load her into the ambulance. Lydia stops and says something to him, and he responds, "I can't Moms. You know I gotta stay here." As they embrace Ted looks over his mother's shoulder and stares at Colm.

Colm diverts his gaze, embarrassed. He looks down the block, where the Animal Services officer grasps the end of a telescopic aluminum pole. At its other end, a small noose has been slipped over the terrier's head. Its bark is now strangled, plaintive, as it struggles to get free.

Ted whirls and watches in disbelief as the Animal Services officer lifts the dog, still trapped in its noose, and slips it into one of the containment cages in the back of the truck, as if he was loading a paddle of bagels into a brick oven. "You bastard!" Ted roars. "You bastard. Give me back my dog." He lunges towards the truck, takes two steps, then stops short as if hitting an invisible wall.

"Ted. Teddy. Edward." Lydia is talking as she tries to pull his elbow. The paramedics have frozen.

"You bastard," Ted yells. "You slimy cocksucker!" The dog-catcher scrambles into the truck, cranks the ignition, and reverses away down the street. Ted swings around and points at Colm. "And you! You are dead. You don't exist. You—" Ted's voice rises to an inarticulate bellow. He turns and punches the side of the ambulance, then punches again, shattering the passenger window.

◼   ◼   ◼

Zelle @ 9 weeks

Zelle cried. She cried at night. She cried in the morning. She cried in the crib in her nursery room. She cried when Colm hummed or Beverly sang. She cried when Colm rocked her in the rocking chair. She cried in the bed, thrashing her tiny body in the space that separated Colm and Beverly. She cried when the neighbour's little dog barked. Zelle cried and cried and cried.

Thanksgiving

—Next year, I'm going to bag a turkey, Len said.

The two couples took a break from the video game. Len sighted along the barrel of the plastic gun-controller that went with the game. He aimed at a small Japanese vase decorated with a painting of birds—bluebirds—on a shelf of knickknacks, beside two framed studio portraits of a young man and a young woman in graduation robes and caps. Elaine and Judy watched.

—Pow, Len said. The trigger spring squeaked against the plastic housing. He snuck a look at Elaine and smirked. Got 'em both. One shot, he said.

—Len's an excellent shot, Judy added. Len had just won ten games in a row of video Duck Hunt, on the Nintendo. Last game he went twenty-two screens without missing a target.

—That pheasant was *terrific*, Elaine said. What a terrific idea for Thanksgiving. Pheasant.

She sucked a long drag from her cigarette, then laid her hand down on the couch so it covered George's lightly. The two fingers holding the cigarette jutted out stiffly at an angle. Smoke curled away from her and George sneezed twice, without covering his face. Some of the ash from the cigarette dropped onto the sofa cover.

—Let me get that, Judy said. She jumped up and scooped the ash into her cupped palm. Very lightly she brushed the sofa, then George's trousers near the knee, where the flesh was bunched in a tight knot beneath the khaki fabric.

—Who's for pie? Judy asked, voice trailing after her as she moved to the kitchen. Pie with liqueurs. Would you like liqueurs? Elaine? George? Len worked the lever to lower the footrest of his La-Z-Boy and eased out of the chair, then ambled over to the dry-bar.

—Don't have to lock this up now that the kids are gone, Len said. He opened the glass doors and tidied the bottles on the shelves, clinking them together and turning the labels to face outwards.

—How about some Amaretto, Len said. Or Frangelica? Hazelnuts.

– Do you have any Grand Marnier, Elaine said. George likes Grand Marnier, don't you, honey. Elaine looked from Len to George and back to Len. She took another drag, leaned over and poked at the ashtray, rolling the cigarette in her fingers so the coal formed a cherry-red, glowing cone. Then she ground it out.

—I like Tia Maria, Elaine said. Do you have Tia Maria, Len?

George quit watching Len sort through the bottles. He picked up a publication from the magazine stand beside the sofa: *Provincial Guide to Game Bird Hunting 1991.*

—How about Sambuca, Len said. Flaming Sambuca. With a coffee bean. You'll like that.

Judy brought a platter in from the kitchen. Four plates with sixth-size pieces of pumpkin pie, the crust over-brown only slightly at the edges. Topped with whipped cream and garnished with Smarties. She put a plate on the coffee table in front of George and another in front of Elaine. She passed out paper napkins.

—This pie is lovely, Elaine said. It looks good enough to eat.

—I hope you like Smarties, Judy said and laughed, covering her mouth. It's real whipped cream, she said. I did it myself.

—I mean it looks too good to eat, Elaine said. Did you get the pumpkin from the garden?

—I forgot the forks, Judy said. We can't eat without forks. She hustled to the sideboard in the dining room and came back with sterling silver pie forks. Grandma's good silver, she said. Len's grandma.

George took a fork and skimmed the whipped cream from his pie and put it in his mouth. The candies crunched as he chewed.

—George, wait for the liqueurs, Elaine said. He put his fork down on the plate, and stared at the pie.

—Honey, get some coffee beans, Len said. The chocolate covered ones.

—Len always makes such a production, Judy said to Elaine, then she looked over at George. George cleared his throat, flipped open the hunting regulations. Judy scurried to the kitchen while Len brought over four small aperitif glasses.

—Don't have proper shooter glasses, Len said, winking at a spot between George and Elaine. But these'll do. I just won't fill them. He set the glasses down, then poured the liqueur. Half-full for Judy and Elaine, to the brim for George and himself. Then he went to the fireplace and retrieved a long wooden match, the kind used to ignite the kindling. George looked up from the page he was reading, leaned over to fetch his drink, and drank it back with a toss of the head. He ran the edge of his thick forefinger across his mouth.

—Hey, hey, Len said, moving his head slightly from side to side. Judy, honey, hurry up with those coffee beans. We're getting antsy in here.

Still standing, Len picked up the bottle to pour George another drink, then hesitated. He put the bottle down. He waited until Judy returned from the kitchen.

—I forgot where I put these, Judy said as she undid a ribbon that held closed a little glassine bag of beans. Santa left these in my stocking last year and I forgot where I stored them, Judy said. I put them in with the Christmas cookie decorations, instead of with the coffee. She fumbled the bag and a bean dropped to the carpet. She dipped down to snatch it up. She polished it with her thumb, then opened the screen to the fireplace and tossed it into the cold hearth.

—We'll have a fire later, Len said, pouring George's drink. Three-quarters full this time. Judy held the top of her blouse closed as she leaned over the coffee table and dropped a bean into each glass.

—Another one, Len said. Two or three each. Let's go to town.

She stood back to watch as Len struck the match against the fieldstone chimney. Cupping his hand to protect the flame, he rolled the lighted match over each drink in turn, until they were all burning with a near-invisible cool-blue fire.

184

—The lights. The lights, Judy said. The room faded to darkness as she gave the dimmer switch a twist.

—Oooooo, said Elaine.

—The alcohol is burning off, George said. With that, he quickly capped his hand over the flame, then drank. He coughed as a coffee bean caught in his throat, then gulped it like a pill. The others watched their drinks flicker for a while, until the chocolate had melted into a slick on the surface of the liquid.

—Time's up, Len said. Like George he capped each drink with his hand. Ouch, he said, shaking it and rubbing his palm. Better let these cool down, ladies, he said.

Judy turned the lights up again. George was eating his pie. It disappeared in four bites. He picked up a whipped-cream-covered Smartie that had fallen in his lap, ran the candy over his bottom lip, then ate it. He closed the hunting regulations booklet and placed it beside his empty plate. On the cover, a mallard duck with an iridescent green head swam placidly in water as smooth as the glass top of the table.

—Pow, George said quietly. He grabbed the book of matches from beside Elaine's package of cigarettes and used a corner of the cover to pick his teeth. Len took a bite from his pie. He spit a Smartie into his hand and put it on his plate with a pile of others he had plucked out of the whipped cream.

—Honey, light the fire now, Len said with his mouth full. He picked up the hunting regulations and leafed through. Next year, I'm going to bag a turkey, Len said.

—The pheasant was terrific, Elaine said. Pheasant. What a good idea.

—Listen to this, Len said, reading from the regulations.

"Merriam's Turkey Special Licences will be issued through a special draw." Blah blah blah. "Application forms and draw envelopes are the same as those used for big game." Big game. Turkey. Oh yeah, Len said. "Each Merriam's Turkey must be tagged immediately after the bird is killed. Tags must remain affixed until the carcass is delivered to the usual residence or to a premises of which there is a Food Establishment Permit issued under the Public Health Act"—All right, that must be a restaurant. I can just see me taking one of these mothers into Earls, and demanding them to cook my turkey, Len said. Ha. Or get this: "Or a Licence for the operation of an Abattoir." That's good. An abattoir. Okay, here we go— "in any case is butchered, cut up and packaged for consumption." What about eating this thing? Listen to this, how to tag it. "For turkey, place wire through nares, or through the patagium." Where do they come up with this stuff, Len said. I'm glad there's pictures here—"between the tendon and bones in the wing."

—It always seems so untidy to me, Judy said. She knelt before the hearth, crinkling newspaper into uniformly sized balls to put at the base of the chimney. I'm glad Len likes to clean the birds as much as he likes to kill them, Judy said.

—I caught a salmon once, in Campbell River, Elaine said. Remember that George? She tore the cover off the matchbook and folded it into quarters, then put it in the pocket of her blouse. She lit a cigarette.

—Sixteen pounds, Elaine said. It made me sad. You enjoyed it though, didn't you, she said to George.

—Oh-oh. There's a gun restriction on these things, Len said. Here it is: "It is unlawful to hunt Merriam's Turkey using a weapon

186

other than a shotgun or a bow and arrow." I'm going to have to try that some time. Bow and arrow. Quiet. Silent like the forest itself. "Or to use a shotgun with a bore diameter smaller than 20 gauge." Rats. I wanted to use my four-ten. It's a real beauty, Len said. Judy, get my four-ten so I can show Elaine and George.

—I hope there's enough kindling here, Judy said.

She lit the paper in the bottom of the chimney to induce a draft. A small puff of smoke drifted into the room. She worked the damper lever back and forth and the paper caught with a whoosh. She lit another of the long matches and ignited a small pile of shavings and sticks stacked tipi-like in the bottom of the fireplace.

—I guess it'll go, Judy said.

Len hopped out of his chair, leaving the footrest up, and disappeared down the corridor. Judy placed a store-bought log made from compressed sawdust atop the small crackling fire.

—Is that one of those that has all the colours? Elaine asked.

Elaine dragged on her cigarette, then made a gesture to remove a piece of tobacco from her lips, even though the cigarette was filter-tipped. As she exhaled a mouthful of smoke, she drew it back in through her nostrils. George's eyes were closed, and he pinched the bridge of his nose. Len came back into the room, carrying a gun cradled in the crook of his arm. He climbed back into the chair and sat down with his legs dangling between the cushion and the still-raised footrest.

—I can't believe I can't use this baby for my turkey, Len said.

—It's, it's, Elaine said. She was staring at the blue metal shotgun barrel. She held her cigarette poised halfway between her knee and her mouth.

—Savage four-ten gauge Over-and-Under, Len said. Art,

almost. Balance. Range. A nice tight pattern. He held his left hand in front of him and described a circle the size of an apple. It's a real piece of work, Len said. He hoisted the shotgun so the shoulder piece nestled against his cheek. He slid his hand along the stock and laid his finger beside the trigger. It's a high-technology hunting machine, Len said. His voice was muffled in the butt of the weapon. He swept the gun around the room, sighting objects along the walls.

—Don't point that thing at me, George said. He ducked and covered his head with his hands.

—Your hands wouldn't provide much protection at this range. Blow 'em clean off. Len didn't look at George when he said this. He was aiming at the china cabinet across the room.

—You shit-for-brains, George said. He ducked lower, sliding off the couch onto his knees.

—George, Elaine said. It's not pointing at you. You're not, are you, Len.

—A little gun-shy, are we, Len said. He aimed above the couch, where George's head had been, and squinted down the barrel. Len relaxed and brought the gun in across his chest, at the military at-arms position.

—Fuck, George said.

—You think I'm such a shit-for-brains, Len said. A firearm is perfectly safe if handled responsibly. You think I'd keep it loaded in the house? You're such a stupid jerk, George. Len held the gun at arm's length and pumped the gun once to show it wasn't loaded. A shell popped free of the breech. It bounced once with a clatter on the glass of the table, then rolled in a semi-circle until it dropped off the edge onto the deep pile of the carpet.

Len looked at the shell, then pumped the gun twice more, but it was empty now. His hands were trembling as he laid the gun on the floor. He leaned back in the chair and hiked his legs onto the footrest. He hugged his knees. George climbed back onto the sofa beside Elaine. He looked at the Elaine's glass of Sambuca but didn't reach for it. He swallowed hard a few times. George wiped his mouth and looked at his hand. Elaine dropped her cigarette, and scrambled to find it among the cushions. After closing the spark screen, Judy unfolded herself from her kneeling position, and brushed and straightened her pantyhose and skirt. She picked up the shotgun shell and looked around for a place to put it.

My father was shot twice, Judy said, rolling the four-ten cartridge in her palm. By accident. I remember as a girl, hunting with my father and brothers by the ponds back of the house. All my cousins and uncles would come for opening day. We'd wait for the twilight, and all the birds—ducks, geese, even swans in those days—would come swooping in low, honking and quacking in big flocks, in threes and fours, alone. Everyone would open up at once, firing at the birds, black silhouettes falling against the dark sky. The ponds were lit in a circle of fire, muzzles flashing. The dogs barking. The smell of burnt gunpowder lifted on the breeze. The spent pellets shot from the other side of the water would rain down on your head, warm and heavy. Once in the side and once in the leg, Judy said. My father. Once by his brother and once by his best friend. You never get shot by accident, by a stranger. It's always someone you know.

She put the shotgun shell onto the plate of pie she had hardly touched, so that it stuck in the whipped cream. She cleared the table, four plates held in one hand, glasses in the other, and went towards the kitchen.

—Who's for coffee? Judy asked.

Tears of the Waiter Soup

The soup is simmered in a broth of tears, shed in a room he forgets. The waiter carries an opaque-green Depression glass mixing bowl. No matter where he goes, even in his sleep, he keeps the bowl in a leather pouch slung over his shoulder. The bowl is with him always. Riding the bus to and from the restaurant, the waiter draws the bowl from its pouch and turns it upside down in his lap to contemplate the inscrutability of the mark etched in its bottom. The waiter runs his gnarled finger, the cracked and misshapen nail gnawed to a nub, over the fluted edges that swirl from base to lip. He wonders, Will I ever fill you again, green bowl?

The waiter cannot know when he will next visit the room. He never remembers that the room exists until he finds himself in it. The first time, he is in the basement of his apartment building, an old tenement constructed in an era when they built in Murphy beds that folded out from the living room walls. He is groping his way through the dim basement corridor to change his laundry over from the washer to the dryer, but he turns left instead of right. Another time, fetching a carton of stemware, he limps up the stairs to the attic storage of the restaurant. He hesitates at the landing and stoops to peer out the small window set too low in the wall. Across the street, in front of an office tower, grows an elm tree that he used to climb when his grandmother lived in a house where the parking garage is now. Instead of continuing up the stairs, he sees a hatch leading under the gable, and enters. Once, searching for a public restroom in a department store, up on the sixth floor behind draperies and floor coverings, next to the credit office where the clicking of knitting needles stopped briefly while the lone woman in the teller's booth watched him, he passed through an unmarked door.

When he walks into the room he forgets, the waiter catches his breath sharply, and squares his shoulders. Light spills into the room, a clean yellow light like the colour of daffodils. A wooden chest in the centre of the room glitters with bright objects. He reaches to withdraw a single shiny key, and he begins to weep. He weeps for the red motorcycle he has never ridden. He catches the tears in the swirling green Depression glass bowl.

Later in the kitchen of the restaurant, the waiter hands the bowl of tears to the chef. The manager scurries to the sidewalk to change the list of daily specials on the blackboard sign. She writes:

Tears of the Waiter Soup!

And anticipates the line-up of the lunchtime crowd. Each sip a red motorcycle when you taste.

Fugue for Solo Cello and Barking Dogs

He trades the boy a hamburger for information. WorldBurger with cheese, no tomatoes, extra pickles. Jumbo fries. Root beer. An ice cream Snowflake for dessert. Robbie eats slowly. Takes a bite, puts the burger down on the styrofoam dish, chews, sips the soda. When the burger's done, the boy picks up stray sesame seeds, licking his finger and pressing down. He opens four packets of salt, builds a hill of NaCl. Rolls each fry in salt before popping it into his mouth. Hamish waits.

Robbie's not supposed to be eating between planned meals and snacks, it throws his blood sugar out of whack. He comes in on a Thursday afternoon, asking for food. Hamish is behind the counter, training a new hire at the soda dispenser. The boy walks up, says, "I know something you don't."

He calls Balvinder, his shift manager, off the prep line to watch the front. While she washes her hands he pours a root beer then steers the boy to the side. He thinks that Robbie's having a reaction. "Hey son, what's up. You all right? Look at me." He checks the eyes for signs of diabetic shock.

"I know something," the boy says.

"What's that?"

"Give me three Double WorldBurgers with cheese, super-jumbo fries and a Snowflake, and I'll tell you."

"What's wrong? Why aren't you in school?" He grabs the pack slung over Robbie's shoulder and roots through it, looking for uneaten food, his tester and insulin kit. The boy's only a couple of months into junior high school, he doesn't go home for lunch any more. He's supposed to watch his own levels.

"Dad, I'm fine. I got out of school 'cause I told them I had a doctor's appointment. That's another thing. You'll have to write me a note."

"What's going on?"

"I know something. I'll tell you what I know, but I want my food first." He thrusts his hands into the pockets of his ball jacket. It's old, got his brother's name on the sleeve, he's tried to blot it out with a laundry marker. Old jeans too, rolled up over sneakers. Hips hung low. He looks at his father through thick lenses.

They move to a booth, away from the order area. A bunch of customers come in. "I want hamburgers and fries and a pop and ice cream."

"I'm calling your mom at home." He stands up.

"She's not there."

"Okay. I'll take you back to school. This is nonsense and you know it." Hamish doesn't know how he'll manage. He rides a bicycle to work, it's a half-hour walk each way there and back. He'll miss the start of the after-school rush.

The boy blurts out: "Kimmy's having sex." The boy's older sister, the man's daughter. She wants to go to Juilliard next year, or Cincinnati. Hamish slumps back down.

"Good grief, Robbie. That's stupid." The palms of his hands start to burn. Hives. He breaks out when he gets nervous. Palms, the backs of the hands, feet, face, scalp. He sweats a lot. It starts like this, with a faint burning. "Who ever told you about sex? When?"

The boy shrugs. Hamish has been through this with two other sons and his daughter. He knows you can't always choose when you have to deliver the birds and the bees, but hopes it's not today, not seated in a plastic booth. Not wearing a uniform, a nametag, a hat with a BurgerWorld logo. Not with a purple plastic dinosaur stuck to his chest. Cross-promotion with TV.

"I want my burgers. And fries. Then I'll tell you more. I've got proof."

"One burger," Hamish says.

"And fries and a Snowflake. Or I won't tell. You won't be able to make me."

When he finishes eating, Robbie pushes his tray aside. Hamish says, "Okay, you've got what you wanted, now finish your game and go home." Throughout the snack he wonders. Kimmy spends all her time studying, practising, rehearsing, playing. A boy from the youth orchestra? A teacher? If it's a teacher, he will go to the police. "Who's Kimmy's boyfriend?" Robbie shrugs. "Who? Is this some trick to get off your diet—" He stops, slaps the table. "Who put you up to this?"

"I wasn't born yesterday, Dad. I know what sex is."

The skin on the backs of Hamish's hands is starting to turn red. Spots appear as if he's been marked with a bingo dauber. Soon welts will erupt. "For god's sake, Robbie." Balvinder and the new hire, Hamish can't remember his name, look over from the cash. Honh the fry cook wanders near the front, wiping his hands on his apron. Hamish has told him a hundred times not to do that. He lowers his voice. "Who told you this? Is this something your brothers put you up to? Did Mike get you to say this? Alan?" He grips Robbie's arm. "Who's telling you these lies?"

"Nobody. Let go of me." The boy squirms away, slouches against the window. He pulls something from an inside pocket of his jacket and puts it on the table.

"What's that?" Hamish says.

"Pills." Birth control pills in a neat little dispenser. A neon-green plastic cover. It's full, a complete cycle.

"Pills?" Voice loud again. Balvinder, the new kid, Honh, even Jason who's supposed to be dedicated to the drive-thru, they're all at the front pretending to do something. A customer glances over, then looks up at the menu board. Others eating at tables are staring. They see the BurgerWorld manager squeezed into a booth with an eleven-year-old boy talking about pills. "He's my son," Hamish says. "Where'd you get these?" His flesh is rising and hardening like biscuit dough.

"Kimmy's room," the boy mumbles.

"When?" His feet are swelling in his shoes, they will soon be itching.

"Sunday."

The Pill. Kimberly.

"Can I have your Barney pin, Dad?"

◼　◼　◼

Dogs follow him home. He pedals through the back lanes and side streets after midnight, and neighbourhood dogs wake from sleep. They stop gnawing rawhide toys. They give up chasing their tails. Ears prick up as the rush of yelps and howls pushes ahead of him like the bow wave of a ship. They raise their snouts to catch the first scent as he rides his bicycle homeward. Terriers squirm through holes in gates. Basset hounds dig under fences. Barkless basenjis leap tall hedges. German shepherds chew through leads, rottweilers snap chains. The man smells like a hamburger. The stink of work covers him, and it drives dogs crazy. A twelve- or fourteen-hour day, noon or earlier till midnight or later, standing behind the grill, slicing onions, frying potatoes, kicking half-eaten KidBurgers from under the tables. His greasy pants, the cuffs of his shirt, the leather of his shoes exude the odours of animal fats and nervous sweat.

He hates dogs. He owns one dog in his life, when he is a boy. A black-and-tan Heinz 57, with mismatched floppy ears and shaggy hair that collects dags. Shane. Shane knows tricks. It delights Hamish and his younger brother Kevin to call "Shane! Come back! Shane!" The dog comes running home. "Porch!"

sends Shane to the nearest doorway. One day, Shane is mating with a neighbour's standard-bred poodle. Kevin commands "Sit!" Shane sits, still stuck to the other dog. Kevin commands "Porch!" The dog hauls his partner across the yard to the back door. Kevin laughs like a hyena but Hamish cries as both dogs yelp in pain. He is dreading that Kevin would call the most clever of Shane's tricks: "Flip!"

Shane likes to fetch and swim. He fetches and swims to death. Springtime, Hamish tosses a stick into the river. "Fetch!" The dog dives in. The stick moves swiftly into the flow of the spring run-off. Shane chases it into fast and deep waters. Fear strikes Hamish. He calls, "Shane! Come back! Shane!" The dog turns, heads upstream into the current. He pumps his legs faster and faster, but still the river carries him away. "Shane! Come back! Shane!" Swells swamp the dog as he bounces from rock to rock. The fast water swallows him, Shane disappears from sight. That was the last time Hamish ever called to a dog. Now they call to him.

He uses the garage door opener strapped to the handlebars beside the headlight to lift the overhead door. There is no room to park a car. Power tools are mounted on workbenches made from old doors and two-by-four trestles. Shelves against the walls and as high as the rafters hold labelled boxes, hand tools, small appliance parts, lumber, electronics, paint, bottles. Garden tools, sports equipment, yard furniture are all stored in a shed outside. In one corner, next to a small water closet and shower behind a folding door, a desk has been outfitted with a computer. Paper reaches up from a box on the floor into a track-feed printer. An ergonomic office chair is tucked under. A framed university diploma hangs above the desk, certifying that Hamish Hamilton has been granted the degree of Bachelor of Science, Honours Geology. Dated 1963, twenty-nine years ago. A row of polished hubcaps decorates one wall. A clothesline stretches across the space, hung with BurgerWorld uniforms.

He sets the kickstand, closes the garage door. The sound of barking fades. He hangs his windbreaker, helmet and cycling gloves on the handlebars, then strips out of his uniform. He tries to convince his brother that he doesn't need the uniform. Kevin is firm: "I own the franchises. But BurgerWorld owns the policies. That's how it's supposed to work. That's what makes me rich, Hammy. Don't fuck with success." Kevin owns a dozen or so BW franchises, all over North America. Just a fraction of the hundreds out there. He's parlayed profits from drug trafficking and the short-order cooking skills learned in prison into a fast food fortune. Clean and sober now. Huge house in Denver. Trophy wife. Concorde to Europe for skiing vacations in the Swiss Alps. Stops for AA meetings in Paris. Met a screenwriter his last time to the Betty Ford, invested in an action-adventure movie that's into its third sequel, he's got some points on the back end.

As he does after every shift, almost every night, Hamish peels out of the clothes, drops them into an old washing machine beside a workbench. He adds some soap, sets the dial, starts it. Helen won't let him in the house with his work clothes. Rancid, she says. He smells rancid. Money, he says, the smell of money. Kimmy gags when she sees and smells his uniform. Loves animals. Vegetarian. Borderline anorexic, he suspects. He wants to ask her if she ever thinks about the horses' hooves melted down for the glue that holds her cello together. About scraping horsehair over sheepguts to make music. About the beetles boiled up to make the shellac that gives it its shine.

Naked, he takes his keys and unlocks a file cabinet. He flips through a stack of magazines with creased covers pulling away from the staple stitch and hidden under an old phone book. *Biker Chix, Rocker Girls, Tattoo Tasties*. He chooses one: *Babes Who Rock'n'Roll*. Feathered hair, little leather vests, wide belts. Straddling Telecaster and Gibson Flying Vee guitars. Bending over Marshall amplifiers. He turns the pages quickly, not lingering until he nears the end. His hand speeds up, he leans over to peer at the small pictures beside the phone sex teasers and dildo ads at the back of the book. He comes with a single grunt, cupping his other palm to catch it, wipes off with a cloth tucked in a box under the bench.

He showers in four minutes, rubs calamine lotion on his brow, his hands, his feet. He pulls on a pair of track pants. A faded sweatshirt, peeling rubberized letters spelling GEOLOGY ALUMNI encircling a university crest.

It's almost one in the morning, but the house is lit up as he crosses the lawn to the back door. Some nights he likes to stand in the yard, watch his house. Following the comings and goings of his family as they move from room to room. Putting lights off and on, pausing at windows where he can tell by their shadow who it is. Tonight the neighbour's dog barks, and he goes right to the back door. Helen sits at the kitchen table, doing paperwork. "I thought that was you," she says when he enters, "I heard Mrs. Klemmer's dog." She fills out an order sheet, makes a note in her accounts book. She sells lingerie at house parties.

"Good night?" Hamish asks.

"Not bad," Helen says. "Mostly nurses, mostly married."

"Where's Kimmy?"

"Downstairs. She got home from rehearsal before me and went to bed hours ago. Robbie was sick tonight, blood sugar's way out. I think he's sneaking food again."

"Was he home alone?"

"Alan was here. Mike's staying over at what's-his-name's."

"On a school night?"

"It's not a school night. Tomorrow's professional development day for teachers. He's going to that basketball camp with Sedge-Serge-Sadji however-you-pronounce-it."

"This family's going to hell in a handbasket." Hamish leafs through the mail in a basket on the counter, then tosses the birth control pills onto the table. Helen doesn't show she notices. She enters some numbers in the calculator, then tears off the tape, staples it in the ledger. She stacks the sheets in a pile. "Where'd you get that?" she asks.

"They're Kimberley's."

"Not what I asked. How'd you get them?" She keeps working.

"You know about this?"

"Of course I knew." She drinks from a half-finished glass. Cuba Libre. Two lime wedges float like dead bugs in the rum and Coke.

"You don't care? You don't tell me?"

"Tell you what?"

"That our daughter's having sex?" Hamish leans against the wall, folds his arms. "Lord, Helen."

"You don't know what you're talking about." Helen closes her books and puts things away in a bulging accordion file. "Sometimes I wonder just how much you do know."

"She's on the Pill, Helen. That means sex. Nookie. Hanky panky. Poosie-dooking."

Helen picks up the order sheets she's done. She drains her drink then goes to the kitchen counter. A fax machine nestles between a canister of sugar and the yellow sharps container for Robbie's used insulin syringes. "Did nearly five-hundred tonight. One woman bought four bras and a corset." She lays the sheets face down, presses a speed dial button.

"Do you know who it is?" Hamish asks. He fiddles with the electric can opener bolted to the wall, presses the lever to rev it a couple of times.

"Mrs. Baxter, Joan, I think her name was."

"Kim's beau." A smoky grey cat appears, lured by the sound that promises open cans. It sniffs his socks, then meows, rubs against his shins.

"She doesn't have one. Where did you get those? Were you looking through her things?" The fax whistles and buzzes as it makes its connection. The first sheet begins its stutter through the machine.

"What if I was. I'm her father. This is still my house."

"If you like snooping around other people's things," Helen says.

Alan walks in from the front room where the sounds of the Second World War blast from the television. Dreadlocks hang in his face. A long-sleeved black T-shirt with an SNFU logo on the front and FUCK YOU printed on the back. Army fatigues with the crotch bagging at the knees. "Are you guys arguing? Can I stay and watch?" Alan says. He doesn't look at either of them, walks between to open the fridge door. "No juice."

"There's some crystals downstairs," Helen says. She pulls a sheet from the fax as it finishes. The next one loads.

Hamish picks up the cat, scratches her ears. "Don't you ever wash your hair?" Hamish says to Alan.

"Ah, the familiar refrain," Alan says. "Dad tells me to get a haircut. Mom, you're supposed to chime in now that I look like a pickaninny." Alan takes a carton of milk, drinks from the spout, burps.

"Get a job and buy your own milk. When I was your age I was going to school full-time, owned my home, kept two jobs."

"Look where that gets you. This is such a cliché. Is this is all we can talk about, haircuts and jobs? What about environmental degradation? What about the politics of the Gulf War?"

"You wouldn't last ten minutes at BW."

"Who'd want to? Besides, I've got a job."

"Planting trees. Watching TV for the other six months of the year and collecting pogey isn't work."

Alan makes a motion with his hand as if to say talk talk talk. He carries the milk to the living room, clicking his tongue stud on his teeth. A voice drones on about the winter of 1941 on the Eastern Front.

"The great communicator," Helen says.

"Who, him or me?"

"Whatever." Helen fixes herself another drink. She pushes her glass into the ice dispenser on the fridge. Rum from the cupboard, Coke from the fridge. She slices a wedge of lime, squeezes the juice into her drink. Drops the wedge in to make three. "You don't get it, do you."

"What is there to get?"

"Kimmy's world-class. She's losing ground here, you know what Maestro Czerny says. He can't teach her anything more."

"Hmph. Czerny. What's that washed-up Polack got to do with Kimmy having sex? It better not be him or I'll tear his smarmy heart out."

Helen looks at her husband for a long moment. She chews an ice cube from her drink. "She should have gone to New York two years ago," she says finally. The fax machine clicks off. She gathers the last of the orders, riffles them in her hand. "They wanted her." She gulps more liquor. "I am so fucking bored with this conversation. You're deliberately not listening. What kind of career will she have if she gets pregnant by accident."

"Career. Career career career, that's all you go on about. Pregnancy's not an accident. She's sixteen."

"If you mention one word of this." Helen picks up the pills from the table. "Don't fuck this up, Hamish. I swear, I won't let you ruin her life."

"What?"

"You figure it out." She goes down the hall to the bedroom. Hamish finds an open tin of food in the fridge and gives some to the cat.

■　■　■

The job interview. The twentieth since Bloody Tuesday at HydroCarbons International (Canada) Inc. more than two years ago. The untruths on the résumé grow bigger: a field geologist, with completions experience. He never worked a day in the field in his twenty-five-plus years at HydroCarb. Fourteen-and-a-half of those years managing inventory and warehousing. He has the best-organized collection of core samples in the Canadian oilpatch, maybe the world. His greatest achievement: writing the specs for the automated logistics and data retrieval system that makes his job expendable. Twenty times he steels himself for the interview. Twenty times he looks in the mirror. Practises his smile. Twenty times he rolls his antiperspirant stick under his arms, over his chest, down his arms, on his neck, his throat. Twenty times he takes antihistamines two days in advance to ward off the itching. Twenty times he sits in the lumpy chair in the reception lobby, reading a two-year-old *Canadian Business*. Twenty times he goes into a stuffy conference room to defend his record at HydroCarb. Twenty times he tries to convince Mr. Smith or Mr. Jones or Mr. Hassan why he is a better candidate than the two hundred or five hundred or two thousand out-of-work professional geologists around town.

Today it's SynerPlus Explorations. Junior oil and gas that has hit on a couple of plays where others gave up. Hamish reads the *Daily Oil Gazette* and *Petroleum Week*: they're an up-and-comer. Looking for field guys. He sits in the lumpy chair. Browses a magazine called *Entrepreneur Success*. He starts to sweat at his collar. His upper lip gleams. The receptionist shows him into the stuffy conference room. A woman enters, hair piled high, drenched in perfume. Her green pantsuit is by a designer Helen could name if she were here. "Mr. Hamilton, I'm Ms. Antonuk. I believe we spoke on the phone."

"Right, you're from H.R." He has been holding a handkerchief in his hand to try to keep it dry, palms it into his jacket pocket, shakes her hand. Hers a desert plain.

"Technically we're not H.R., we have an industrial psychology practice."

"Great."

"We're running a little late, Mr. Hamilton, so if you have no objections, I'll get right down to business." She looks up. "Do you want some water or a coffee?"

Hamish clears his throat. "No." The pads of his hands below the thumbs start to burn.

She opens a legal-size folder. Hamish's name is on the tab, a blue sticker stuck below it. She makes a note on a piece of paper. "I'm going to ask you to fill out this profile survey. It helps us build a background and give us a sense of how the candidate can benefit the team. When you're done, Mr. Chiang and Mr. Musselman from SynerPlus will come in and ask you a few questions." She looks up again.

Hamish looks back. "You're not with SynerPlus?"

"No, I'm consulting for them." Hamish continues to look at her. He recognizes her now from the last days at HydroCarb. She plays both sides of the human resources game. He wants to ask, You bill out at, what, one-twenty-five an hour? One-fifty? "Shall we proceed, then?" Two hundred?

"Right. Let's do it," says Hamish. He wipes his chin and brow.

"Before we get to the survey," Ms. Antonuk picks up a paper from the folder and begins to read: "Let me state for the record, on behalf of SynerPlus Exploration Ltd., that the position of

Exploration Geologist will be filled by a candidate who is: between the ages of eighteen and sixty-five; legally entitled to work in Canada; physically fit to perform the functions of the position which may include, but not be limited to, long hours in an office environment or at a well site, travel, and lifting under twenty-two kilograms; willing to undergo a pre-employment medical examination conducted by a physician of the company's choosing; willing to submit to urinalysis as a condition of pre-employment and at any other time the company may request it; and who agrees to full disclosure in security background investigations including disclosure of criminal convictions, pending criminal or civil actions, business holdings, partnerships or any other financial dealings that represent a fiduciary duty, or any other aspect of character, conduct or personal history that the company may legally request; in possession of a valid permit to operate a motor vehicle."

"Great," Hamish says. "I'm legal, capable. Fit as a fiddle. Drug-free. My life's an open book, and I can drive. Yes to all."

"You aren't required to respond to any of this information." Ms. Antonuk makes another note as she speaks. "How long?"

"Pardon," Hamish says.

"How long drug-free?"

"Forever. I've never touched drugs."

"Never? No personal history?"

Mother on Valium, brother on speed and cocaine, wife on Prozac, a son smoking pot. Daughter on the Pill. "Never taken any."

Ms. Antonuk writes some more. "Never any prescription medication, nothing over-the-counter, no aspirin, Tylenol."

"Oh sure. Penicillin a few times. Cold and flu stuff. Cough drops."

"Antidepressants, tranquilizers, barbiturates."

"No. Just antihistamines." He holds his hands under the table, scratches the backs until they almost bleed.

More notes in her file. She hands a small booklet to him. "This is the profile survey. Most candidates take about fifteen minutes to complete it. Any questions?"

"Pen or pencil?"

"You choose," she says. "You're on your own." As she goes out the door, she presses a button on her watch.

Hamish checks his own watch. Is fifteen minutes the mean or the median? Is the time to finish the questionnaire part of the test? Examines his writing tools: a BurgerWorld ballpoint with a plastic cap, and the mechanical pencil from the set he received for his HydroCarb twenty-year award. Pencil. He rushes through the questions, answering what he thinks they're looking for. A couple he mulls over.

What was the last book you read?

He's been reading biographic profiles at the library when he's supposed to be researching oilpatch jobs. About self-made millionaires. Not books. Magazine articles, entries in almanacs. Travelling salesman King Gillette invents the safety razor, the design comes to him in flash when he's shaving. Harland Sanders turns chickens into dollar bills. Ron Popiel makes a fortune from the Pocket Fisherman and the Veg-O-Matic. Just in the lobby he's read about Joseph Cossman—sells a million dollars worth of spud guns from the backs of comic books.

Hamish answers the question with the titles of books he's never read: Sun Tzu's *Art of War*, and *Swimming with the Sharks*. His fingers begin to swell with the stress hives. Writing nearly illegible.

Choose the statement that best describes you:
__ I like to balance my life and my work
__ I like to work until the job's done
__ I believe in an honest day's work for an honest day's pay

He marks the middle choice, changes his mind for the first. The eraser on his pencil is hard and brittle. He licks it, rubs at the mark on the page, tearing the paper.

Choose the statement that best describes you:
__ I am a team player
__ I am a leader
__ I am an independent thinker

He marks an X beside the first choice, it's obviously the answer they're looking for. Writes in, very faintly, a question of his own: Why can't someone be all three? He doesn't think he's that person.

When he finishes the thirty questions, he checks his watch. Just under fourteen minutes. Ms. Antonuk enters. "All done?" He hands her the paper. She scans it for a few seconds, then slides it into the folder. There is a red label now stuck next to the blue one. "I'll just run off a copy of this and be back in a moment with Mr. Musselman and Mr. Chiang." She steps out.

Hamish pulls the handkerchief from his pocket, wipes his brow and chin. He runs a finger around his collar. The flesh on his forehead feels as hard as saddle leather. His feet are popping out of his shoes. She returns with the two men, introduces them. Both men are younger than Hamish by at least ten years. Sharp-edged tailored suits, silk ties, crisp white shirts. Mr. Musselman wipes his hand on his trouser leg after shaking hands.

Hamish's inner ears begin to itch, his Eustachian tubes boil. He grinds a finger in one ear, then the other. One of the men asks a question about explorations experience. A yellow label has joined the red and blue on Ms. Antonuk's folder.

"Excuse me." Hamish says.

"Are you all right?" Mr. Chiang asks. He looks up from the paper he is examining. Someone else's résumé.

"I'm a hard worker. I love to work."

"Good. That's good. Field work means long hours. As I'm sure you know."

"You should see my house," Hamish hauls himself to his feet. Mr. Musselman looks at Mr. Chiang. Ms. Antonuk shuffles the papers in front of her, makes a note in a box.

"I'll just be going now." Hamish lurches through the door. On his way out, he grabs the magazine from the lobby. There is a profile of a man who built a watch-repair empire. He spills into the street. Gulps the air. He is not sure if he needs to laugh or vomit. He has a plan. He is finished with job interviews.

◼   ◼   ◼

Bang! The garage door rattles as one of the boys outside drills a shot wide, and the hard rubber road-hockey ball makes contact. Clatter of sticks. "Centre it! Shoot!" Bang! The door rattles again.

Hamish pulls down the Christmas decorations from the rafters of the garage. He lives on a street famous for its annual displays. Hamish is one of four neighbours who started it. For years he makes all the street's snowmen and candy canes in his garage. But the neighbourhood changes. Families come and go. Not everyone celebrates Christmas anymore. He wipes down his snowman, touches up the sign with black paint. "Merry Xmas from the Hamiltons." He and Helen argue for years whether they need an apostrophe. He runs the strings of lights down the floor, replaces the burned bulbs.

It's warm inside. He burns lumber ends and salvaged wood in a small Franklin stove, and there's a gas space heater. He builds this garage with his own hands, Hamish and Helen's dad Ion. Seventeen years ago. Helen pregnant with Kimmy. His own dad pitches in as best he can, hollering advice from the lawn chair. It's the summer he's dying of cancer. Mesothelioma. Nobody can understand how a tobacco-hating produce manager at a grocery store contracts a lung cancer associated to asbestos and smoking. Ion and Hamish barely exchange a word. Helen translates the Romanian when she needs to. Strong as two oxen. Stubborn. Nine days to put the garage in. Not all the finishes. But the walls, trusses, roofing, electrical rough-in, plumbing. They think he's nuts to have spent all the time beforehand hand-trenching the water and sewer, who has a bathroom in the garage? He never regrets it. The city will never make him take it out. Adds value to the property. That's the name of the game. Improve your property.

Shouts in the driveway, the sound of a scuffle, sticks quiet. Hamish hears his son Mike's voice: "Hold him down."

Robbie: "Fuck off, Mike."

Mike: "Hold him still, I said."

Sajjad: "Isn't your dad in there?"

Robbie: "You cunt. I'll never do it. Even if you make me."

Mike: "We'll see about that." [*Thumps and slaps. Grunting.*]

Sajjad: "Isn't your dad in there?" [*Robbie whimpers.*] "Shit. Oh shit."

Mike: "Don't let him go or you're next."

Sajjad: "Fuck me. What if your dad—"

Mike: "My dad doesn't give a shit. He's probably jerking off. Hey!" [*Running feet alongside the garage.*] "You fuckwad. Why'd you let go."

Robbie [*Yelling from the other side of the garage.*]: "Never. You'll never make me do it. You stupid dink."

Sajjad: "You're crazy."

Hamish turns on the table saw. Rips some two-by-four lengths into thin laths. He needs to shore up Santa's reindeer. He's still got lumber left over from all the renos. The first year after he's laid off, he rebuilds and refinishes the whole place. Twenty-seven years at HydroCarb minding his business. He estimates the renovations add forty, maybe even forty-eight thousand to the value of the house, though materials' cost to him is under twenty.

He does all the labour. Best materials. Except for the roof—he uses a contractor for the roof—six guys from Newfoundland take three days for the whole job. Nine thousand, but a roof is a roof. Good for another twenty years. He owns it all free and clear, no mortgage, no line of credit. Everything he owns is free and clear. House, car, appliances. Even Kimmy's cello. It's worth almost as much as the house. Well, maybe half as much. Commits to it

214

when she is ten, Czerny says she needs an instrument to match her gifts. Czerny finds it, he's got contacts all over the world. Some Austrian family that needs the cash. Pays probably seventy-five percent of what it could get at auction, Czerny doesn't take any commission. Hamish has to finance it, but pays it out when he gets his HydroCarb package. By the end of year one after the downsizing, with renovations complete and cello purchased, the savings are all gone. But he owns everything free and clear. Managing BurgerWorld keeps all the balls in the air.

He puts the finishing touches on Rudolph, arranges the decorations on the floor. Tomorrow's a Sunday, he'll be home all day. He'll set them up outside. After putting his tools away, sweeping and tidying, he prepares for work. He irons one of his uniforms, puts it on. Before he puts on his parka and mitts and pedals into the afternoon, he sits at his desk, unlocks his file cabinet. He wonders about Mike's comment: how can he know about the magazines in the bottom drawer? Or was it just a figure of speech?

Hamish pulls folders from a different drawer. Franchise information packages for Subway, KFC, BurgerWorld, Tim Hortons, a bagel place, coffee, Chinese food, pizza, ten others. Even McDonald's, the franchisee's holy grail.

Fast food is hard work. Hamish can tell as soon he goes into another store, sometimes just driving by, he can tell if the manager gets it. Best to check when business is dead, the lull between breakfast and lunch. Cleanliness and activity. In a couple of seconds he can clock those two things, know whether the food's good. Whether the owner is seeing any return. If it's 11 a.m. and there are no customers, and still trays to be bussed, still finger marks on the glass doors, the kids are in the back snapping towels, forget about it. It's hard work. Hamish is there six days a week, sometimes seven if he has to cover a shift.

People who work for Hamish work hard. He doesn't hire kids if he can help it. The immigrants are good, except language. He's careful not to hire too many from one circle. Not that it's ever been a problem. But he hears stories. One bad apple, it goes to hell. He mixes it up. Balvinder is his right arm, he'd hire ten of her for any job on the planet. She's a complainer, but she gets it done. Honh is always there, logs more hours than even Hamish, but he's untrainable.

People come into the store from HydroCarb. Guys he used to work with, some are still there. They do a double take. Hamish lets them think it's his franchise. He's keeping the bills paid, he's doing all right. Kevin's BurgerWorld has become the top-performing store in Western Canada since Hamish started as manager. He's even cracked the Canadian top five a couple of times. Kevin looks after him, he's looking after Kevin.

But maybe he can do better for himself.

Each folder he pulls from the cabinet has a worksheet clipped to the front, a table listing capital, assets, sources of credit, potential returns and income. At the bottom of each worksheet are two underlined numbers. The first number is potential annual income. The second is the cash he needs to buy in. With the best of franchises, that's what you need. No loans. Not even from family. Cash. He brings a folder to the top. Affordability versus profitability. His future is donuts.

◨　◨　◨

He crouches in the fresh snow, looking through the basement windows of his own house. The flakes accumulate on his shoulders and hat. His knees begin to ache from the crouch. He knows when he stands up his right hip will be stiff. Yet he continues to peek. There are two windows along the side of the house. Scuttling back and forth he can see most of the basement. In the long finished front room, Kimberly sits astride the cello. Quarter-profile, her right side and shoulder. Her hair is pulled into a tight ponytail, its almost-white blonde contrasting with the black turtleneck sweater. Black turtleneck and black tights, the only thing she wears outside of performance. That hair she brushes out a hundred times each night. For years when she was a little girl he sat beside her to count out the strokes. When did he quit doing that? Why? Is it gradually, or all at once? Over her shoulder on the music stand, he can see the score she is learning. The notes drift up through the glass. One of those modern pieces, fast, technical. He doesn't understand it. He is so proud of her, what she can do. When she plays in concert, the audience hangs in rapt attention. Complete strangers weep when she plays, it makes him cry too because they are crying, because his daughter's playing makes them cry. He is so proud. Yet he can feel his cheeks start to tingle with shame. He adores his Kimmy, he is awed by her talent. But he has never been able to overcome his indifference to the actual music. Supple and firm, her hand glides up and down the neck of the cello. Her other hand draws the bow back and forth in sure, fluid strokes. It dips and dives, stops suddenly as she plays a short passage *pizzicato*.

He moves to the other window. Helen is in the semi-finished laundry and workroom. Wearing her housecoat, sorting her inventory on a long table. Most of it boxed or packaged, but every once in a while she picks up a merry widow or a pair of stockings that are loose, folds them. As Hamish watches, she undoes the belt, shrugs the housecoat from her shoulders. She is naked except for a garter belt that rests low on her hips, holding up silk stockings. She looks over, almost at him. Hamish draws back. Then he knows she is looking the in mirror on the wall below and a little to one side of the window. She smoothes the folds of the stockings over her thighs, adjusts a garter. She turns side to side, looks over her shoulder.

She is almost ten years younger than Hamish. He has worked to stay in shape, rides his bike, watches his diet, but his skin grows slack, bags accumulate under his eyes. Helen still has smooth olive skin. She cups her small rounded breasts, holds them up against their slight sag. Her nipples are stiff in the centre of the dark brown aureoles. Her stomach plumps in a slight curve, he can just see the two lightning bolts of the pregnancy stretch marks and the crescent moon of Robbie's caesarean scar. Thick thighs frame her dark pubic patch. She slips into a brassiere from a box on the table. Hamish pays attention to her body for the first time in weeks. She is the only woman in the world he ever holds close to his own body, the only woman in the world he makes love to, the only woman he has ever loved. He watches her pull on a pair of panties, two skimpy triangles of silk. She checks herself in the reflection. Tucking here, rearranging there. Her body is a mystery he learns over eight thousand nights. Sleeping side by side, scratching her back, bathing her feet. Holding the belly swelling in pregnancy, watching as she opens her womb to let the world swallow her children. He learns her mystery as a witness to its change. And now this, this woman in lace and silk. She never dresses in this lingerie for him, he never asks her to. He sees her as other men see her, as a lover might.

The back door opens and closes in the house next door. He hears the jingle of collar and licence at the fence behind him. The neighbour's dog growls, presses its snout through a crack between boards. Hamish looks behind, sees teeth as the dog snarls. "Shoo," he says. The dog growls again. Hamish's knees pop as he straightens up. "Easy, boy," he says to the dog. The dog barks. Hamish breaks into a run, in his peripheral vision he thinks he sees Helen move to the window, thinks he hears the cello stop playing. As he moves to the back, the dog follows on the other side, barking and scratching at the fence. He drops a mitt, fumbles for his keys at the door to the garage, locks himself inside. He hears Mrs. Klemmer calling to her dog, "Heidi! Heidi. Vass is das?" He stands inside the door, holds his breath, feels his beating heart. His hands sting.

■   ■   ■

He calls a family meeting one morning, before school. They cram themselves around the kitchen table. "When was the last time we were all at the table at the same time?" Robbie asks. He pushes Shredded Wheat around his bowl with his spoon. He answers himself: "Probably last Christmas."

Mike is eating his way through a stack of toast gobbed with peanut butter. Fingers clutch a pen as he copies something from one notebook to another. Headphones clapped over his ears, the thumping bassline, rap vocals. Bent head bobs to the beat. Alan slouches in a chair, blows on a cup of tea. Leans back, closes his eyes.

Helen babysits a stack of paper in the fax document feeder. "Oh no, it was sooner than that. That's almost a year ago. Easter at least. Didn't we have that barbecue last summer?"

"Barbecues don't count," Robbie says. "We're all in the yard, but not at the table."

"Thanksgiving dinner?"

"I was away Thanksgiving," Kimmy says. She peels a banana, slices it into her organic yogurt and granola. She pulls one of the books away from Mike. "Hey, that's my book. What are you doing?"

Mike pulls it back. "I need that."

"You loser, you're copying my homework. That's two years old."

Robbie speaks up: "Mike says Mrs. Boyle's still handing out the same assignments. He says I'll be able to use it too."

"Pathetic. Hey," she says. She reaches over, yanks the headphones from Mike's ears. "That book was in my room. Did you go in my room?" Mike keeps his head down, copies more homework. "Mom, Mike went in my room." She snaps the phones back. Mike slides them down on his shoulders, stops the tape.

"What's the big deal. Everyone else does."

"What's that supposed to mean?"

Mike shrugs. "Ask Dad."

She turns to her father. "What's he talking about. You go in my room too? I told you, Mom. I told you. I'm getting a lock."

Hamish speaks: "There will be no locks on any doors in this house."

220

"But—"

"No buts. No locks. End of discussion." Spoons clink against the rims of bowls, Alan slurps, Mike's pen scratches. The fax completes its transmission with a beep. Hamish clears his throat.

Robbie says, "You have a lock on the garage."

"That's different."

"Why?" Robbie holds a spoonful of cereal in mid-air, waits for an answer. Mike and Alan exchange smirks. Kimmy nibbles her yogurt. "Why is it different?"

Hamish's face turns red. He rubs his cheeks. Sweat forms on his upper lip. Helen intercedes: "I don't think your dad asked us all together to talk about locks and doors. Let's save that discussion for another day." She comes up behind Robbie, massages his shoulders.

"When?"

"Later," Helen says.

Hamish clears his throat again. A hive the size of a horsefly bite bulges on the end of his nose. "I thought we should have a little meeting so I could let everyone know about some things I've been giving a lot of thought to."

"Is this gonna be long, because I gotta leave to catch my bus in like nine minutes." Mike closes the books.

"We'll see how long it takes and you stay right in your chair."

"Okay, okay. You're the one who has the big hairy about being late and missing classes."

"I'll drive you if you miss the bus," Helen says.

"Mike's got a point. I don't have to be to school till ten, but I can't sit around all morning. I want to practise."

"Enough! We will sit at this table until I say so. You too,

Helen. Sit." Helen is back over by the sink. She pours a coffee, stands to one side. "I've been thinking about a lot of things. The future. What's best for us. The family. I've decided we need to change some things."

Helen: "Don't you think we should talk about this first?"

"Just listen, Helen. I've thought long and hard. I've decided to face the facts. I realize I need to change careers." He stops. Waits.

Robbie: "You're not going to work at BurgerWorld anymore?"

"No. I mean geology. I'm not going to be a geologist any more."

Alan stirs from his slouch. "Gee, Dad, no offence, but that's a no-brainer. I mean, what's it been? Three years?"

"Twenty-eight-and-a-half months."

Helen: "Where are you going with this?"

Mike: "Yeah, Pops, what's up?"

"I've been at BurgerWorld a couple of years and I've learned a great deal about the fast food industry—"

Helen groans, puts her cup down.

"—I've seen your Uncle Kevin have great success leveraging his capital—"

Helen: "Don't do this, Hamish. You can still stop."

"—and I see no reason why we can't be successful too—"

"I knew it. I knew it."

"—It would be an excellent opportunity for the whole family—"

"I can't believe this. I can't believe you never once asked my opinion."

"—to participate and help out and earn a little money too. What do you think?"

Silence. Helen shakes her head. Five pairs of eyes avoid his gaze. Finally Robbie says, "What do you mean, Dad?"

"He means," Kimmy says, "that he wants to own his own restaurant serving up dead cows and dead pigs and dead chickens."

"Cool," says Mike.

"And he wants us all to work there like some sort of family slave labour."

"Oh. Not so cool."

Hamish clears his throat again. He rubs at his nose. His fingers feel like Italian sausages swelling and burning with their own heat. His nose feels like a foot stuck to his face. "Not burgers." He flips open the file folder face down in front of him, pulls out a brochure. "Donuts. Tim Hortons Donuts."

Robbie: "Wow."

Helen: "And how do you propose to pay for this, the dutiful wife asks, dreading the answer that she thinks she already knows."

"We'll take out a mortgage on the house."

"Okay, I'll bite. Will that give you enough for a Tim Hortons?"

"Well, no. In point of fact, it won't. We'll need to come up with some more."

"Borrow it? Are you going to ask Kevin for help?"

"Well, no. They don't like partnerships. A family loan would be construed as partnership. Franchisers like to see liquidity. Unencumbered cash."

"And where do you suppose we'll find cash of the sort you're talking, let alone unencumbered?"

"We'll have to be creative. Look for assets with a value. Think of how we have to create a value proposition."

"Cut the crap. Like what?" Helen presses.

Kimmy jumps in: "You're talking about my cello, aren't you?" Hamish doesn't answer right away. "You are. You're going to sell my cello. Say it."

"Well—"

"No." Kimmy says, almost whispering. "No. You can't. I won't let you."

"Yes," Mike says, punching the air with his fist. "Say good-bye to Mr. Mozart, hello, Mr. Horton."

"No." Kimmy says. She raises her voice, but still speaks without shouting, enunciating every word. "You loser fuck—"

Helen stops her. "It's okay. It's okay, Kay-Kay. I told you I won't let him."

Alan gets up from his chair smiling, shakes his head. "Oh man. Dad, I knew you were twisted, but this—man, this is out there." He goes to Kimmy, whispers something in his sister's ear. She snorts, laughing through the tears she's not letting out. Alan walks away into the living room.

Mike crams the last half piece of toast in his mouth, bolts his orange juice. "Hey, it's been a slice, but I gotta run. Don't think I'll be getting that ride after all." He puts his headphones on, cranks the music, scoops up the notebooks. Out the door in fifteen seconds, coat in hand, shoes flapping, bag on back.

"You will not do this," Helen says.

"We need to. We need to thrive. Money doesn't grow on trees. You need to work for it. Sacrifice. Take risks. Build something."

"I hate you." Kimmy turns to confront him. Her nostrils flare with contained anger. "I hate you. Mom's right, you're just jealous. You're a pathetic failure and you want everyone else to be too. You're all just jealous." She pushes Helen's hand away, goes to the basement. The sound of her bedroom door slamming crashes up the stairs.

"You couldn't think to talk about this. I've seen this coming for weeks. You couldn't bear to ask me about this because you knew I'd say no. Is that all you see when you watch her play? Dollar signs? Is that all it means to you?"

Hamish is silent. The cat sits on his lap. When did she jump up? There she is, sitting in his lap, looking up at him. Music filters from the stereo in Kimmy's room. Beethoven. Even Hamish recognizes that. Television sounds drift in from the living room. A voice-over describes the American carpet-bombing of the Ho Chi Minh Trail. Hamish's nose throbs. He wants to pound it with his fists.

"Talk about future and change, you go ahead. Talk all you want." Helen shakes her finger, it trembles. "Be prepared. Because I can talk too." She clears the dishes from the table, clatters them together. Stomps on the treadle to make the trash can lid pop open. She scrapes uneaten food into the garbage, loads the dishwasher, banging the cutlery and glassware. She empties the dregs of the coffee into the sink, rinses the pot. The fax beeps to tell her she's received something. She tears the thermal paper out of the machine. Scans the fax, crumples it into a ball and puts it in her pocket. She goes to the top of the stairs, turns to Hamish. "I'll show you a fucking future, you prick." Helen goes to her daughter.

Hamish and Robbie are left at the table. "I'll work in the donut shop, Dad."

"Thanks, Robbie. Thank you."

"I gotta get ready for school."

"Sure, ready for school. Don't forget your insulin."

"I won't." Robbie goes to the fridge, takes a bottle of insulin from the door. He gets his test kit and a syringe from the cupboard.

"Do you need any help?"

"No, I can do it, Dad." Robbie goes down the hall to the bathroom, shuts the door.

Hamish sits alone, strokes the cat. She stretches her legs up onto his chest. Her purring vibrates against his belly, her claws prick him as she kneads his shirt. He imagines speaking to the cat. It's all mine, he imagines saying. My house, my kitchen, my fridge, my table. He imagines he goes into the living room, throws Alan into the street. My couch, my television, my remote control. He imagines he sits beside Mike on the yellow school bus, strips off the headphones. My Walkman. He imagines he walks downstairs into Kimmy's room. My cello. He imagines he takes the cello into the garage. My garage. He imagines them all banging at the windows and the doors, begging him to come out, to give up. He imagines his tools. My hammer, my sixteen-ounce Stanley framing hammer. He imagines he pounds the cello to pieces. He imagines he feeds the splinters into his Franklin stove, the two-hundred-year-old varnish cracking and popping, the dry wood burning to a white-hot ash. He imagines he holds his face and hands close to the fire. He imagines the heat soothes his itch. "Imagine that," he says to the cat. My cat.

Wrestlemania

The numbers wouldn't add up. "They made a mistake on my T-4 slip," Colm said.

Beverly stood by the kitchen door, coat on, purse over arm. "I doubt it," she said. The television on the counter flickered with the images of two bulky men colliding with each other and falling down. The sound was off.

"You misplaced one of my pay stubs," Colm said. He sorted through the neat stacks of paper on the table. "I'm missing February fifteenth to twenty-ninth. Last year was a leap year." He punched numbers into the adding machine and carefully examined the results that printed on the narrow tape. "This calculator is malfunctioning," he said.

"I'm going to pick up the kids," Beverly said.

"Who?"

"The kids. The two small people who live here. Your son and daughter. You declare them as dependants on page three."

"Not any more," Colm said.

"What?" Beverly said.

"You don't declare children any more. They changed the rules years ago. You get a child tax credit. But it's all wrong." Colm watched a bald man rant on the television. He ran a hand over his own balding head and remembered the formula for a sphere. "You're leaving me. You go to pick up the children and you don't come back." He licked his pencil and entered a number on the form.

"I think sometimes that's what you want."

"I wouldn't blame you," Colm said. He licked his pencil again.

"Why do you do that," Beverly said. "Lick your pencil. I'm going to Gaddie's to pick up Zelle and Will."

"You'll smoke in the car," Colm said.

Bent over, her head stuck in the closet as she rummaged in the shoes, Beverly replied, "I don't smoke, Colm. It's you who used to sneak cigarettes in the car. Have you seen my rubber boots?"

"You'll be gone two hours. Enough time to see another man." He broke the lead off the pencil, watched the end skitter away onto the linoleum floor. He put the pencil into a sharpener shaped like a small globe of the world. On TV, an obese Asian man costumed like a Sumo wrestler sat on a man wearing sequined lavender tights. Colm examined the map on the sharpener and said: "They put Japan in the wrong place." He tested the new point on the arborite tabletop, pressing down harder and harder until the lead broke off again.

Beverly walked in her boots across the kitchen and took a package from the freezer compartment of the refrigerator. "Can you pick up the table when you're done?" she said.

228

"It's tax time," Colm said. "Do you love me still?"

"Yes, Colm," Beverly said, and opened the door into the rain. "Still." She closed the door after her.

"Still," Colm repeated. "Come back," he said to the closed door. He picked up the remote control and increased the volume. The crowd screamed and the canvas thudded drum-like as wrestlers fell. "Wrestling is fixed," Colm said.

Towards a Semiosis of Two-headed Dog

Box

A plain wooden box. Pine. Not a coffin. Bigger than a breadbox. Footlocker. Address stencilled. Customs clearance affixed. Contains:

Square black bag

Surgical implements: bone saw, rib spreaders, suture needles

Trumpet

Jewellery box with mother-of-pearl cufflinks

Waterman fountain pen with gold nib

Wire-rimmed spectacles

Military cap with oak leaf
Freemason apron
Hand-tinted photo of baby, naked on white fur rug
Snapshot: mother, wife and daughter under magnolia tree
Baseball glove (old fashioned with no pocket)
Gas mask
Fleece-lined slippers worn through the sole
Jazz records. Bill Evans. MJQ. Two dozen Miles.
    Ornette Coleman. Bix and Louis on 78s, Dizzy, Duke,
    the Count. Ella, Django Reinhardt. Trane. Bird.
The Harvard Medical Library, Volume III of the Recorded
    Lecture Series, 1952; includes interview "Experimental
    Transplant Surgery in the Soviet Union"

Imagine This

Soviet scientists, circa 1951, transplant the head of one dog onto the body of another. You learn this from a long-playing record found among your father's possessions, right beside *Sketches of Spain*. You sit rocking in your favourite chair watching the record go around, stylus unwinding the two-language groove, Russian interpreted by BBC English. Sandy, faithful Sandy, curls at your feet, sleeping through his species' holocaust historiography.

Head Graft

"We grafted the head of an Alsatian to the neck of another, attaching it just above the shoulders near the second vertebra. Naturally there was no neurological response in the second head, but we did ensure the circulation of blood . . . Both heads remained alive for almost forty-eight hours, at which time we performed autopsies . . .

"We also conducted heart and lung transplants and liver transplants on dogs and pigs. The subjects were maintained in a vital state for up to seventy hours . . . The potential for kidney transplants excites us. Subject pigs with functioning kidney transplants are alive to this day."

Photos

He looks so soft in the baby photo. Hair—even then he had thick black hair—slicked back in the same style he would wear for the next seventy-four years. The hand-tinting lends his flesh a bright rosy colour, unnatural, but somehow more healthy than the swarthy jaundiced yellow he had as a father. The smile. Did he ever smile?

And the snapshot: Mother, wife and daughter, three generations of women beneath a magnolia. They are like aliens. Mother has grown smaller, has let her hair go white and plain. Wife is the same, eyes smouldering, hand planted provocatively on hip. Daughter almost an adult, she'll be starting college next year, too beautiful, looks away from the camera, stares upwards at something over her head exposing the long slope of her throat. The Georgia sunshine falls on them, broken by the leaves above. The photo is recent: on the back, written in his hand grown spidery with age but still recognizable, is a date from just over a year ago. It unsettles me to think that there, a half a continent away, he took this picture that now even a year later shows them new to me.

Favourite dogs

A note written with a quick flowing hand. The purple run of faded ink from a fountain pen. The paper: the backs of two pages ripped from a desk calendar dated March 27 and 28, 1962. Found inside the sleeve of the Harvard Medical Lectures:

> Two favourite dogs in literature from the Odyssey and Olaf Stapledon. Odysseus's dog what was his name? Waits 20 yrs for master to return. Sick among houseful of conniving suitors he recognizes O. tho dressed as beggar. Raises head 1 last time, sniffs hand then dies as only Homer makes death. How much better a dog than 3 headed hell hound! Olaf's dog—can't remember if named Cerberus or Sirius—from '30s sci-fi, read it as a boy. Dog with human brain transplant. Very funny, touching. No one understands him. Eventually kills master and runs with wolves. (Argus = O.'s dog.)

To M, to W, to D

to walk with you in the bright of noon, in our parents' dark, in the uneven break of dawn, to walk along the water's edge, the cold black water of night running a river, we walk so close I can smell your skin beneath the waves of wind, first you then I move ahead fall behind out of step, the flowing river sucking at the shore, a glance, a glancing brush of forearms, goosefleshed breeze along the river, we walk and the river flows and we walk and the river flows and the river flows, and we walk and our hands, put your hand, you put mine, we put hands, and the river flows and our hands held, not clasped, fingers not interlocking, and the river flows and your hand paper-dry holding mine, your hand warm and fleshy fitting tight, your hand light and soft flitting on my palm and a dog, a yellow dog, a golden retriever named Sandy, our dogs always yellow, always golden retrievers named Sandy, swims in the current to catch a stick and scrambles up the bank, shaking off from tail to head, splashing, and the river . . .

Understanding father

He developed chemical weapons at the Suffield Military Weapons Range during World War II. He ran away from there, to Atlanta. I ran back, to Alberta.

I take a deep sniff from his army cap, trying to smell something—there is only the camphor stink of mothballs. I finger the Freemason apron. Close my eyes, listening for cryptic messages. I spread all the things from the box on the carpet before me.

When I blow the trumpet only a harsh blat issues forth—one of the spit valves is missing. The twisted brass is like a gleaming intestine, and I think of his last hours as the peritonitis festered in the ulcers in his bowel. I lay the horn down on the Freemason apron, mouthpiece at the top, bell down. One by one I pick up the pieces of his life and arrange them, constructing a father. I position the cap, floating it above a head-spaced emptiness. For his right arm, the two photos, placed askew to approximate an elbow. The right hand the baseball glove. I place the canister of the gas mask at his left shoulder, the hose trails as his arm, the mask at the end serves as his left hand. The surgical instruments and black bag become the bones of his legs, the slippers his feet. The pen and cufflinks are penis and testicles.

I put a stack of Miles on the turntable. First to cue is Live in Paris with Tadd Dameron, 1949. I remove the black vinyl disc of the Harvard Medical Lectures and place it as the head of my father, then spread the wire-rim spectacles across where the bridge of his nose would be.

Then I lie down at an angle, so that my head touches his, just above the shoulder. I watch the ceiling. I can hear Sandy barking in the back yard, almost in time to be-bop.

W. Mark Giles's fiction and other writing have appeared in magazines and papers across the country, including *The Malahat Review, Geist, The New Quarterly, NeWest Review, Grain, subTerrain, The Antigonish Review* and *Canadian Fiction Magazine*. Mark currently lives in Calgary.